Ben looked like a thunderbolt had hit him. He loved her.

He loved them both. Benjy. His son. And Lily.

He always had, he thought, and it was such a massive lightbulb moment that he felt his world shift in some momentous way that he didn't understand.

But his world hadn't moved from its axis. It was as if it had settled back onto an axis that he hadn't known was missing.

His son had needed him and he'd been there. If Benjy needed him again, how could he not be close?

If Lily needed him... It was exactly the same.

And more. He thought then that it was more than him being needed. Because what he felt for them both was a need itself.

He needed them both. They might need him, but he needed them so desperately that he could never aga

Today he'd bee
there for Lily a
and ever, as lon

He needed them

Marion Lennox was born on an Australian dairy farm. She moved on—mostly because the cows weren't interested in her stories! Marion writes Medical Romance™ as well as Romance™. Initially she used different names, so if you're looking for past books, search also for author Trisha David. In her non-writing life Marion cares (haphazardly) for her husband, kids, dogs, cats, chickens and anyone else who lines up at her dinner table. She fights her rampant garden (she's losing) and her house dust (she's lost!). She also travels, which she finds seriously addictive. As a teenager Marion was told she'd never get anywhere reading romance. Now romance is the basis of her stories, her stories allow her to travel, and if ever there was one advertisement for following your dream, she'd be it! You can contact Marion at www.marionlennox.com

Recent titles by the same author:

RESCUE AT CRADLE LAKE
THE HEIR'S CHOSEN BRIDE
  (*Castle at Dolphin Bay*)*
THE DOCTOR'S PROPOSAL
  (*Castle at Dolphin Bay*)
HIS SECRET LOVE-CHILD
  (*Crocodile Creek*)

*Mills & Boon® Romance™

THE SURGEON'S FAMILY MIRACLE

BY

MARION LENNOX

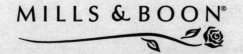

MILLS & BOON®

First published in Great Britain 2006
Paperback edition 2007
Harlequin Mills & Boon Limited,
Eton House, 18-24 Paradise Road, Richmond, Surrey TW9 1SR

© Marion Lennox 2006

ISBN-13: 978 0 263 85219 6
ISBN-10:   0 263 85219 9

Set in Times Roman 10¼ on 12 pt
03-0207-51574

Printed and bound in Spain
by Litografia Rosés, S.A., Barcelona

THE SURGEON'S FAMILY MIRACLE

PROLOGUE

LILY stared at the thin blue line in consternation. Her plane ticket was right beside her on the bed. In three hours she'd be flying back to Kapua, her Pacific island home, and from now on she and Ben would be nothing but friends.

She was pregnant.

She gazed at herself in the mirror, horror building. They'd been so careful for the past four years, but last week she'd had a tummy bug, and this week, knowing she might never see him again... Well, the only sure contraceptive was abstinence and how could she bear to be apart if this final week was all she had?

She was having Ben's baby.

She needed to tell him.

The thought made her blench. He'd hate it. She knew how much he'd hate it. Ben who held himself aloof, who backed away at the first sign of need—how could he be a father? Maybe the biggest reason he'd let himself be drawn into their relationship had been that at the end of four years he'd known she had to go home.

She loved him with all her heart.

She closed her eyes, overwhelmed with panic. How could she leave him, knowing she was carrying his child? How could she leave him at all?

He wouldn't let her leave if he knew she was pregnant. She knew that about him. He might hold himself apart; he might admit he needed no one; but her lovely Ben was an honourable man. He'd suffered a desperately lonely childhood himself, and to have a child grow up without a father… He wouldn't do it.

But neither could he love a child, she thought bleakly. He didn't know what loving was. They'd been together now for almost all their medical training, and for all that time her loving had been a one-way deal.

Oh, she couldn't complain. Ben had been honest with her from the start. 'Lily, I love you as much as I'll ever love a woman, but I don't want a permanent relationship.' He'd spelt it out repeatedly, making sure she'd understood. 'This time together is great, but as soon as we finish medical school I need to go and see the world.'

But now…

Ben would feel the same about abortion as she did, she thought, but anything else… She'd seen the flare of panic whenever she'd come close to admitting she needed him, and a child would make no difference. Or maybe it would make him decide to marry her, she thought bleakly, and that would be worse than loneliness. He'd be trapped by his own sense of decency.

The clock ticked on. She should be packing.

Ben didn't need her, she told herself. He didn't need anyone. And back home in Kapua, her fellow islanders truly did. She continued staring into the mirror, thinking of the girl she'd been ten minutes ago and the woman she'd suddenly become.

She was a woman with obligations.

Kapua, her island home since she was eight years old, had never had a doctor. Islanders were dying because of it. But Lily had excelled at school, and she'd been desperate to study medicine. Somehow the islanders had supported that wish. Kapua's economy was subsistence level, which meant the islanders' decision to fund her medical training had been huge. Her family and neighbours had gone without basic necessities to give her—and themselves—this chance.

The further her training had progressed, the more the islanders' anticipation had built. Their telephone calls over the last few months had been jubilant. They'd built a hospital because they knew she was coming. She was qualified. The island would have its first doctor.

She was carrying Ben's child.

Appalled, she let the test strip fall and her hand dropped to her waistline. She was feeling for a pregnancy that was hardly there. This was so new. So tiny. A fragment of human life.

Pregnancy didn't always end in a live birth, she thought, trying not to cry. To tell Ben now…

Impossible. He was off at the end of this week on his first mission with the armed forces. He'd react with forcefulness, she thought. He'd decide on marriage. He'd organise a date for a wedding during his first leave.

But if she left—as she had to leave—he wouldn't follow, she thought bleakly. She'd tried so hard to persuade him to visit her island but he'd reacted with incomprehension. The islanders were her family? How could that be? He didn't know what a family was.

Family…. Yes, the islanders were her family. They'd love this child to bits, she thought.

Ben would see a child as nothing more than chains.

She was rocking back and forth now, distressed beyond measure. How could she tell him? If she told him then he'd insist on marriage, and how could she refuse him? But how could she not go home?

'So tell him and go anyway,' she told her reflection.

'I'm not brave enough.'

There were footsteps on the outside stairs. The door was

flung open, and Ben was there. Her lovely Ben. Big and strong and tanned, and laughing for the sheer joy of living.

The father of her child.

'Lily, they've accepted me into SAS training,' he said before she could say a word, and he was across the room, lifting her, swinging her round and round in his excitement. 'It's the crack army assault team—the best in the world. You'll be off saving your little island but I'll be seeing the world.' He spun her round and round until she felt dizzy, and when he finally set her on her feet she had no choice but to lean against him, to feel the strength of him one last time.

'Sweetheart, we've each achieved our dream,' he said, and she could tell that his thoughts were already off in the exciting future where she played no part. 'I'll miss you like hell, my love.'

'I'll miss you,' she managed, but only just.

'Will you?' He cupped her chin, forcing her to look at him, but his eyes were alive with excitement, and he didn't see the change in hers.

'I can't understand how you can want to go back to such a place as Kapua,' he said. 'When the whole world is yours.'

'The island is my world.'

He nodded. 'I guess,' he said, hugging her against him. 'I guess we're both driven, but in different directions. But I wish we could share.'

'No, you don't,' she whispered, but so softly he didn't hear. She whispered it from her heart to his. 'You don't wish we could share, my love. You're my darling Ben Blayden—who walks alone.'

CHAPTER ONE

'ISN'T Kapua where Lily Cyprano lives?'

Ben was running to a tight schedule, and he sighed as Sam Hopper joined him. Sam was a skilled surgeon but he talked too much. The first Chinook was leaving in an hour. Normally the adrenalin was kicking in by now, making him move with lightning speed, but lately... Hell, what did it mean when preparation for disaster seemed routine?

'What?' he asked without looking up, and Sam poured himself coffee and hiked his frame onto the bench where Ben was sorting drugs.

'Lily,' he repeated patiently. 'Cute as a button. Half islander, half French. We all thought she looked like Audrey Hepburn, only curvier. Sexiest thing on two legs. She went through med school, then went home to work on the little island where she'd been raised. Wasn't that Kapua?' He paused, sorting old memories. 'Hey, weren't you two an item? I was a couple of years above you but I seem to remember... I'm right, aren't I?'

Ben's hands stilled. For a moment—just for a moment—a surge of remembered pain washed through him. Lily.

Then he regrouped. 'We're talking about seven years ago,' he snapped. 'The trivia you keep in that tiny mind of yours...'

'But Kapua is Lily's island?'

'Yeah,' Ben said, remembering. He'd been so caught up in the urgency of the job that until now he hadn't thought of the link between Kapua and Lily. But, yes, Kapua was definitely the place Lily called home.

'Is she still there?'

'How would I know? I haven't heard from her for years.'

'It'd be a joke if she was among the insurgents.'

'A great joke,' he said dryly, starting to pack again.

They were moving fast. News had hit that morning of an insurgent attack in Kapua. The islanders needed help, desperately.

Kapua was the biggest of a small group of Pacific islands. Its population was an interracial mix of the original Polynesians and the Spaniards who'd decided to colonise the place centuries ago. There was little sign of that colonisation now. The Spaniards had obviously decided the Polynesian lifestyle suited them much better than their own, and the island's laid-back lifestyle continued to this day.

But things were changing. Ignored by the rest of the world for centuries, the island had recently been made more interesting to other countries by the discovery of oil. The island's rulers had shown minimal interest in selling it. To sell the oil could change their lifestyle, but it would leave their descendants without resources when it was finished. The islanders had therefore decided to make the oil last maybe a hundred years or more, and so far they'd sold nothing.

That decision seemed to suit most islanders, but greed did dreadful things. It took few brains to guess that the insurgents who'd stormed the capital would be interested in only one thing—oil money.

'It's just as well the island has big friends,' Sam said, moving on, and Ben nodded. The call for help had been frantic. The insurgents had blasted their way into Kapua's council compound, and there were reports of deaths and chaos across the island. This wasn't a political take-over where oil wealth would be shared among the whole population. The opinion of those who knew was that this would be a group with outside backing—backing that could potentially cause instability in the entire Pacific region.

With such destruction—with human loss and chaos—there was little choice for Kapua's political allies. Troops were therefore flying in immediately. Among them would be Lieutenant Ben Blayden, M.D.

She's probably forgotten me, he thought grimly. What's the bet she'll be a fat island mama by now, with six or seven kids?

That thought made him smile. Domesticity would have made Lily happy. All through her medical training she'd ached to be home.

'My island's family to me,' she'd told him. 'Come and see what it's like.'

Not him. He was in too much of a hurry to get where he wanted, and he wanted action. The thought of settling on a remote island and raising children made him shudder.

But Lily...

'Lily was great,' he told Sam. 'She was a good-looking lady.'

'Look her up when you get there.'

'Pop in and make a social call during the gunfire?'

'Maybe it's not as serious as reported,' Sam said optimistically. 'Maybe you can persuade the nasty men to put away their guns, pour margueritas for everyone and go lie on the beach.'

'As if.'

'You never know,' Sam said, yawning. 'But at least it'll be action. See if you can find a few bodies that need sewing up. Nice interesting cases. I'll be there in a flash.'

'You want to take my place?'

'After you persuade the boys to put their guns away,' Sam said, grinning. 'You're the front-line doctor. Not me.'

* * *

'I can't find Benjy.'

Lily was making her way through the crowded hospital, terror making her numb. All around her were people who needed her. The criminals who'd taken over the compound had shot indiscriminately, seeming to relish the destruction they were creating. The death count at the moment stood at twenty but there were scores of injured, scores of people Lily should be caring for right now.

But Benjy…

At first sign of trouble, when Kapua's finance councillor had stumbled through Lily's front door that morning, clutching her bloodied arm, Lily had told Benjy to run to Kira's house.

Kira was Lily's great-aunt, a loving, gentle lady who was like a grandmother to Benjy. She lived well away from the town centre, in an island-style bure by the beach. Benjy would be safe there, Lily had thought as she'd worked her way through the chaos of that morning.

Then, at midday, an elderly man had stumbled into the hospital, weeping. Kira's neighbour.

'Kira,' the man had wept. 'Kira.'

Somehow Lily had finished treating an islander she'd been working on. A bullet had penetrated the man's thigh, causing massive tissue damage. He'd need further surgery but for the moment the bleeding had been controlled. As soon as she'd been able to step away from the table she'd run, to find that Kira's hut had been burned, to find Kira dead and to find no sign of her son.

She'd stood on the beach and looked at the carnage and felt sick to the stomach. Dear God…

Where was her little boy? Nowhere. By the time she returned to the hospital she was shaking so badly that her chief nurse took control, holding her arms in his broad hands and giving her a gentle shake.

'What do you mean, you can't find Benjy? Isn't he with Kira?'

'Kira's dead. Shot in the back, Pieter. That kind, loving old lady. And Benjy's gone. There's no one on the beach at all.' Her breath caught on a sob of terror. 'Where would he have gone? Why isn't he here?' She was close to collapse, and the big islander pushed her into a chair, knelt before her and took both her hands in his.

'Maybe he's with Jacques.'

'I don't know where Jacques is either. Oh, God, if he's…' She buried her face in her hands.

But Pieter was hauling her hands down, meeting her gaze head on. He was the island's most senior nurse, sixty or so, big and gentle and as patient as any man she'd met. The look of fear in his eyes now made her more terrified than she'd been in her life. If Pieter was scared…

But he had himself more together than she did. 'So Benjy's probably with Jacques,' he told her. 'Or he'll be hiding. It's a good sign, Lily. Benjy's the most sensible six-year-old I know. If we look for him or for Jacques, it'll only jeopardise us all. You were crazy to have left the hospital yourself.'

He hesitated then, but they had to face facts. 'I'm sorry, but you need to block Benjy out, Lily. You're our only doctor and we need you. Trust Jacques to take care of him. For now Benjy's on his own and so are we.'

It was dusk as the Chinook carrying Ben hovered over the northern beach, its searchlights illuminating the sweep of sand while they assessed whether it was safe to land.

'We have the north beach secured,' they'd been told on a shaky radio connection by a deputy head of council who'd seemed to be having trouble speaking. 'They don't seem to be near. And the hospital's ours. That's all.'

A problem with an idyllic island existence, thought Ben grimly, was that it left everyone exposed to the nasties of this world. Life in paradise is all very well if everyone feels that way. The majority of islanders hadn't owned guns. They'd never dreamed of needing them and it had left the way for the few to run riot.

A burst of gunfire came from their left and the pilot swung the Chinook round so the floodlights pierced the forest.

'That's M16s,' the sergeant sitting beside Ben told them. 'I recognise the firing pattern. They sound too far away to be accurate. Reports are that most of these guys were already on the ground. We're therefore acting on the assumption that they won't have high-calibre weapons. They'll give us trouble on the ground but if that's all they have… I say land.'

'OK, we're going in,' the pilot said. 'You know your job, guys. Let's go.'

Pieter had personally brought another two units of plasma into the operating theatre. He was needed outside, Lily knew, but she also knew he was treating her as a patient—a patient who he needed to stay on her feet. The woman under her hands was the island's housing councillor. The wound to her chest was deep and ugly. It was a miracle the shot had missed her heart. All Lily's attention had to be on her, but Pieter knew that she needed at least some hope.

He was giving it to her now.

'Friendly troops are landing on Fringe Beach,' he said. 'A couple of new patients have come in from the rainforest and they saw them land. We've radioed for help and it's come.'

Lily was hardly listening. 'Benjy,' she was whispering over and over again. 'Benjy…'

'How many?' one of the theatre nurses asked, and Lily focused enough to hear terror in her voice that matched her own. Any minute now the few armed men they had could be subdued. The insurgents could take this place over.

And outside… Somewhere in this island was her six-year-old son.

'Three helicopters so far.'

Lily could feel a tiny lessening of terror in the theatre staff at the news. Outside help?

'These men are cowards,' Pieter said into the stillness. 'They've left this place alone because they know we have guns here. They'll shoot us but they won't risk being shot themselves. They won't have counted on outside help so soon. I'm guessing they hoped to bring more military supplies—maybe more men—onto the island before that.'

'If they're not already here…'

'If they had full military capability, they'd have shot down the helicopters,' Pieter said soundly and Lily thought, Benjy, Benjy, Benjy.

'Many of the islanders are hiding,' Pieter added, glancing at her. 'Long may they stay hidden.'

Benjy.

'Is there any news from the council compound?' a nurse asked, and Lily clamped off a blood vessel and waited for the site to be swabbed. She felt sick.

'We don't know what's happened there,' Pieter said. 'All we know is that those who ran from the building were shot.'

'Were those inside shot, too?'

'Who would know?' Pieter said heavily. 'There's no access. Anyone who goes near the place is met with gunfire.' He handed over the plasma, glanced at Lily to see if she was OK—was anyone OK just now?—and turned away.

'There are three more urgent cases,' he told Lily dully. 'Hand over here as soon as you can.'

She worked all that night and into the next morning, blocking out everything but medical imperatives. Or she almost blocked out everything. There was so much need. They needed a dozen doctors and there was only her. She worked like an automaton, her silent plea a background throbbing that could never stop.

Benjy, Benjy, Benjy.

'You need to sleep,' Pieter told her at four in the morning, and she shook her head.

'How can I sleep?'

'I feel the same. But we're no good to anyone if we collapse.'

'We're good until we collapse,' Lily said bleakly, turning to the next stretcher. A burst of gunfire in the distance made her wince. 'That's the way it's going to be.'

It was almost dawn. There were two platoons with full military and medical gear on the ground now, brought in under cover of darkness. Crack SAS troops, with more on the way.

'How can they hope to have had a successful coup?' Ben demanded. He was treating a corporal who'd been hit in the face. A bullet aimed at him had hit a tree and sheared off what had essentially been an arrow. The man's face was grazed, and once the splinter was out he'd be fine. If this was the extent of their casualties, they'd be lucky.

'The guess is that they'd never expect us to act this quickly,' the corporal told him. 'First rule of warfare—never mess with a country who shares our passion for cricket.'

The man left and Ben rechecked his gear. As soon as the island was secured they could search for wounded, but for now, when the road into the township was still under insurgent hands, there was time to think.

About Lily?

Ever since Sam's comment yesterday she'd been drifting in and out of his mind. At such a time, with her medical training, she had to be at the hospital. When could they reach the hospital?

He worked on, sorting gear so that when they moved into the township the urgent stuff could be moved first and he wouldn't be left without imperative supplies. His job was partly about good medicine, but it was also a lot about good organisation.

'Hey, Doc, we've got the road clear,' a voice called, and he turned to see a corporal emerge from the shadows. Graham was a sometime paramedic, depending on need. 'I've just been talking to the big boys,' he said. 'We're heading for the hospital now. It seems to have become a refuge. The locals we've found are saying there's been a recent drug problem on the island, so the hospital orderlies have been trained to be security guards. The first insurgents got a reception of gunfire and they've left the place alone. That's where our initial radio report came from and we're in contact with the radio operator now. He's telling us it's safe to come in.'

Lily, Ben thought.

She wasn't necessarily at the hospital, he told himself. She could be anywhere. He glanced across at the few canvas-shrouded figures on the beach. She could even be…

Don't go there.

Dawn. She was still operating, but without much hope. They were out of plasma, low on everything, and the child under her hands had lost so much blood that she almost hadn't started operating. But therein lay defeat and somewhere in the back of her exhausted mind lay a cold fury that had grown so great that if any of the insurgents had been close to her scalpel right this minute, they would have feared for their lives.

The boy she was operating on—Henri—was a friend of Benjy's. Three nights ago she'd made pizza for the pair of them and they'd watched a silly movie, she in the middle of the settee, with a little boy at either side.

Henri had been with his father on the beach where Kira had been killed. Henri's father had fled with the wounded boy into the rainforest and had waited far too long before he dared bring the boy for treatment.

Benjy and Henri…

'I'm sorry. I didn't see what happened to Benjy,' Henri's father had told her, but all his attention had been on his son, and Lily's must, be too.

The wound on Henri's thigh was massive, tissue torn clear and jagged fragments of bone embedded in what remained. It was well beyond Lily's area of expertise. She was sweating as she worked, and as she looked at the heart monitor and saw that she was failing, she knew tears were mixing with the sweat.

Damn them. Damn them, damn them, damn them.

Then the door slammed open. The theatre staff jerked to attention. In truth they'd spent the last twenty four hours expecting gunmen to burst in, and these were gunmen—but they were dressed in khaki uniforms she recognised. Friends.

'Keep still, everyone,' drawled a voice as armed men, pointed machine-guns and the officer in command assessed what was before him. Checking that the place wasn't an insurgent stronghold. But here was no disguising that a very real operation was taking place. There was also no disguising that they were operating on a child. The officer in charge made a lightning assessment and obviously decided this was no place for warfare. 'Who's in charge?' he said, and Lily checked the monitor, winced again and managed to reply.

'I'm operating. This child is critical. We have to continue.'

'What do you need, Doctor?' he asked, and her heart, which had almost stopped beating, started to thump again.

'Plasma,' she said, and she made no attempt to disguise the desperation in her voice. 'Now. And help. If you have anyone with medical training…'

'Right.' This was a man of few words and plenty of action and Lily blessed him for it. 'Everyone out except theatre staff. Let's keep this place as aseptic as possible. Someone find the medical supplies now, and get Ben in here, pronto.'

The machine-guns disappeared. Lily turned her attention to the wound again as the door slammed open once more.

'Plasma's on its way,' a voice said. 'I'm a doctor. Do you want me to scrub?'

She didn't look up. She couldn't. 'Yes, please,' she managed, and the man hauled off his outer uniform, let it fall to the floor and crossed to the sinks.

'Lily's exhausted,' Pieter told him. 'She's been operating for almost twenty-four hours and her hands are shaking.'

'That's what I'm here for,' the voice said. 'More medics are on their way but I'm the forerunner. I'm a Lieutenant in the SAS, and I have surgical training. What do you want me to do?'

'Ben,' Lily whispered, and she lifted her hands clear. Her fingers were trembling so much she couldn't go on.

'Doctor,' Pieter said urgently, and magically Ben was there, lifting the clamps from Lily's fingers and checking the monitor.

'Get that plasma here now,' he roared in a voice that could be heard in the middle of next week. He glanced at Pieter, who was acting as anaesthetist. 'Are you a doctor?'

'I'm a nurse with the basic training Lily's taught me. I'm Pieter.'

'Then, Lily, you take over the anaesthetic,' Ben snapped. 'Pieter, no offence but...'

'Of course there's no offence,' Pieter said, motioning to Lily to take over. 'If you knew how pleased I am to leave this to you guys...'

'I can imagine,' Ben said, and fixed his gaze on Lily, forcing her to steady. 'You can do this,' he said.

She took a deep breath. 'I can.'

'Right,' he snapped. 'Don't you dare collapse. There's no time. Let's get this kid out of danger and worry about everything else later.'

Ben was there.

She was so exhausted she could hardly think, but the knowledge settled in her heart and stayed. It made her feel…not better but somehow less hopeless.

Which was crazy. It was ridiculous to think that Ben Blayden could make all right with her world. Though he'd thought so from the start. He was loud and bossy and sure that his way was right.

'There are no easy answers,' she'd told him at the end of med school. They'd been discussing their future, but they'd already accepted their future didn't involve each other.

'Of course there are easy answers. You follow your vocation and you don't get distracted,' he'd said, and she'd wanted to agree with him but she hadn't been able to. She had already been distracted.

And now here he was again, just as distracting. She could hardly see him under his mask and theatre cap, but she'd glimpsed enough to see that he'd hardly changed. Still with that mass of jet-black curls that always looked unruly, that always looked supremely sexy. Still with those deep brown eyes, creased at the edges from constant laughter. Still with that body that said he worked hard and he played hard, strongly physical.

Ben was just who they needed right now.

He'd always been just who she needed.

'Blood pressure,' he snapped, and she responded fast, the medical side of her working once more on automatic.

'Seventy on forty-five.'

'We're clamping this and waiting,' he snapped. 'There's muck further down but to clear it involves further blood loss. We have to get that pressure up first.'

Muck further down…

She'd never intended to clear it. The bullet that had smashed into Henri had obviously blasted though wood first, as there were shards of splintered timber in the wound. She'd decided her only option was to get the bleeding vessels clamped and the wound closed, then hope like hell they could get him off the island to a competent surgeon before the wound festered.

Now here was Ben, saying let's take our time, let's use the plasma, get his blood pressure up and get this wound properly cleaned.

The tiny frisson of hope built, both for Henri and for them all.

He wouldn't operate this way unless he knew that things weren't hopeless outside, she thought. He wasn't closing fast and moving on to the next disaster.

Right. She firmed and made her tired mind find its third or fourth or maybe its twentieth wind. She could do this.

'Thank you, Ben,' she whispered, and he flashed her a look of concern.

She looked away. She didn't need sympathy now. If he said just one word… Her world could collapse, she thought.

Dear God, where was Benjy?

Now that Henri's blood pressure was rising Ben worked swiftly, knowing the anaesthetic itself was a strain on this desperately injured child. But now they had plasma he thought he'd make it. The child was strong and otherwise healthy, and Lily had done the hard part.

Lily.

This was no contented mama with six or seven babies. He glanced along the table to where she stood at Henri's head. All he could see of her was her eyes. They were the same eyes he'd fallen hard for more than ten years before, when they had still been kids at university. But they'd changed. She seemed haunted. She looked exhausted beyond all limits, exhausted by something that went beyond this present drama.

If he'd had another doctor he'd have ordered her away from the table. Even if she wanted to work, having such an exhausted colleague had its own risks. But the rest of the medical team wasn't flying in until they were sure it was safe to do so. Ben was the forerunner, sent to deal with frontline casualties, and there'd be no more medics here for the next few hours.

So he worked on, and Lily watched Henri's obs like a hawk, and monitored the anaesthetic as if she'd been trained to the job.

She'd been practising here for seven years, Ben thought. She'd been a lone doctor here for seven years. She'd need so many skills…

She'd fall over if he didn't hurry.

'I'm closing now,' he said at last, and saw Lily's shoulders sag under her theatre gown. Was it just exhaustion?

'Before I came here I did a rough check of the wards,' he told her, trying to alleviate a terror he only sensed. 'Unless more have come in, there's nothing else urgent. The rest of my medical team will probably be here in the next few hours. Why don't I take over and you guys get some sleep?'

'We won't sleep,' Pieter said gruffly, speaking for them all. 'We don't know what's gone on outside. Until we know what's happened to the rest of the islanders, there'll be no sleep for anyone.'

Lily was reversing the anaesthetic. Henri coughed and gagged his way into consciousness and as soon as he did so she stepped away from the table.

'I need to go.'

'Stay,' Ben said urgently. 'I need to talk to you.'

'There's no outstanding surgery?'

'Not as far as I know, but—'

'I'm sorry Ben,' she faltered, looking down at Henri. Maybe

she was thinking she should stay. But her gaze moved to Ben and her shoulders straightened. 'I have to go. Now. Please, look after him. Pieter, will you talk to his father?'

'Of course we will,' Pieter said, and he put his hands on Lily's shoulders and propelled her out of the room. 'You go,' he said. 'And find him safe.'

Who was she worried about?

He couldn't follow. It was a complex wound and dressing it took time. Then he worked out antibiotic doses and started them running through the drip. Then the moment he walked out the door he was clutched by a man who turned out to be Henri's father.

'Is he…?'

'He'll be fine,' Ben said gently. 'As I'm sure Lily told you. You can see him in a minute. Just take that shirt off first, will you?' He grimaced at the gore over the man's clothes. He'd carried his desperately injured son to the hospital and it showed. 'You'll scare Henri into a relapse if he sees you like that.' Then, as the man's terror didn't fade, he took him by the arm and led him into the theatre. Henri was still coming round. There were tubes going everywhere, but his breathing was strong and steady and colour was seeping back into his face.

'He's not quite awake,' Ben said. 'Change your shirt and you can sit with him while he wakes.'

'His mother,' the man muttered.

Ben thought, Uh-oh, and braced himself for another tragedy. But it seemed none was coming.

'His mother's in Sydney,' he whispered. 'My daughter's won a scholarship to boarding school there. Our daughter's very clever, you know. She's fourteen and she's…' He broke off and buried his face in his hands.

'Let me give you something to help the trembling,' Ben said, even though all he wanted to do right now was find Lily. 'I want…'

'We all want, mate,' Ben said softly. 'Let's just do what comes next.'

What came next—treating him for shock and dressing a jagged cut across his elbow that the man hadn't noticed until Ben helped him off with his shirt—took time. Then, just as he'd settled Henri's dad into a chair by Henri's bedside and wondered who'd sleep the deepest, a private came to find him.

'One of our men's got a flash burn to the arm,' he told him. 'They're chucking out Molotov cocktails and he got hit.'

'From where?'

'From that place they call the council compound.' He shrugged. 'We're mopping up now—there doesn't seem to be any aggressive fire from anywhere else on the island except from there. Paul was just real unlucky to be hit.'

'So what's happening?' Ben asked. 'Did our guys storm the place?'

'Dunno about that,' the private told him, leading the way back to his friend with the burns. 'They're saying there are hostages. The sergeant reckons when they saw how many of us had arrived they took fright, grabbed as many people as they could and barricaded themselves in. The powers that be have had us fall back out of range. My mate here's the last one injured. We sit and wait, Sarge reckons.'

They'd reached his mate now, a lanky corporal with an arm that was blistered and raw. 'Ouch,' Ben said. 'You've been playing with matches?'

The corporal gave him a sickly grin and Ben looked round to find Pieter, anyone, to prepare him a syringe of morphine.

Pieter appeared as if he'd known he was being looked for. His face, though, was more grim than the last time Ben had seen it.

'What's up?' he asked.

'I hope not much,' Pieter said. 'My wife and daughters are

OK. Word is that order's being restored, except at the council compound.'

'Do we know how many people are in there?'

'I have no idea,' Pieter said brusquely. 'Lily's gone to find out.'

'Lily…' Ben frowned. 'She might be needed here. If she's anywhere else, she ought to be asleep.'

'You can't expect that of her,' Pieter said. 'Her son's missing and her fiancé. They've been missing for twenty-four hours now and Lily's going out of her mind.'

CHAPTER TWO

HE WAS caught for the next few hours. At mid morning the roads were declared open. A no go area was declared around the complex of buildings called the Council Compound—a series of bungalows surrounding a palm filled conclave used for island gatherings. Here the insurgents had holed up. There was no clear idea how many were there, or who was insurgent and who was hostage, but a cursory sweep had now been made of the entire island. The insurgents were either laying down their arms and declaring this had been a mistake, or they were with their comrades in the compound.

It had surely been a mistake, Ben thought grimly as more injured made their way to the hospital.

Where was Lily? He couldn't leave the hospital.

At midday a plane landed on the island's small airstrip, bringing Ben's colleagues—people like Sam, who relished trauma surgery. Ben's role was hands on if necessary but it was mostly organisational, getting on the ground first, assessing what was needed, doing hands-on treatment in the first few hours but then handing over to those more qualified in various specialties. These guys were good and their arrival meant he could often stand aside.

Not today. There was too much to be done. There was a

sports oval beside the island's hospital. The hospital was tiny, totally inadequate to cope with the influx of wounded. Four hours after the arrival of his team and equipment Ben had a massive field hospital erected as an annexe. Operating theatres, a triage centre, ward beds… They'd erected this hospital before and his team knew their stuff.

As well as the hospital itself there was the need to organise supplies. Was there enough plasma? Were there enough body bags?

Would he ever get used to this? Ben wondered, as he worked on into the afternoon.

These were Lily's people.

Where was she? Every time anyone approached he looked up, hoping it was her.

She'd be aware that she was no longer desperately needed. She'd be searching for her son and for her fiancé.

Her son and her fiancé.

Well, he'd expected her to be married with babies. Why did those two words have the capacity to make him feel as if he'd been kicked?

It was only because he didn't know where she was, he told himself as the day progressed. It was only because he couldn't help her.

He was helping her now, doing her work for her.

He wanted, quite desperately, to find her.

Finally, as dusk was falling, the bulk of the organisational work had been done and the urgent cases had been treated. It was time to hand over. Sam was available to take charge.

'I'm taking some sleep,' he told Sam, and Sam looked down to where Ben was changing his theatre slippers for military boots.

'Sleeping quarters for med staff are right through the canvas,' Sam said cautiously. 'You're expecting to die with your boots on?'

'There's no threat.'

'So you're putting your boots on, why?'

'I'm taking a walk.'

'To take in the sights,' Sam said, smiling. They'd worked together for a long time now, and Sam knew him well. 'You've been on your feet since last night. You're dropping where you stand. But you're going for a walk.'

'No one knows where Lily is.'

Sam's smile faded. 'Our Lily?'

'She was here when I first arrived,' Ben said. 'She was close to collapse when I arrived but her kid's missing.'

'Her kid.' Sam's brow creased. 'What sort of kid?'

'How the hell would I know? A kid kid. Pieter—the head nurse—told me she's got a kid she can't find but Pieter's gone home and won't be back on duty till tomorrow. I can't find anyone who knows where she is so I'm taking a look.'

'Grab some men,' Sam told him. 'There's lurgies out in that dark forest.'

He wasn't kidding. There was rainforest everywhere. Who knew what rebels were still out there, wanting to…?

Kill Lily?

It was a dumb thought, brought about by exhaustion, but even so the thought wouldn't go away. He felt sick.

'I'll be careful,' he told Sam.

'You want me to come with you and hold your hand?'

'You're afraid of the dark.'

'There is that,' Sam said peaceably, with just the faintest rueful grin to show Ben wasn't far off the mark. 'But for the gorgeous Lily…I'll risk it.'

'Look, she's an old friend and she's in trouble,' Ben said, exasperated. 'Unless you have any more dumb comments, you're holding me back.'

'Off you go, then,' Sam said, standing aside. He'd almost

been laughing but as Ben rose from lacing his boots Sam put a hand on his shoulder. There was a long line of grim reminders out the back of the hospital, reminding them both just how serious this situation was.

'Find her,' he said.

Dusk had given way to darkness when Ben made it to the road leading to the compound. He'd been hailed three times on the way.

'Ben, this lady's got a kid who got badly mosquito bitten while they were hiding.'

'Ben, I reckon I'm allergic to the water. You got something to settle my stomach?'

And finally the worst, which was: 'Ben, we've found another body. You want to come and take a look before we shift it to the morgue?'

It didn't make sense, Ben thought. The insurgents had appeared at dawn and had stormed toward the compound, shooting everything in their path. If they'd hoped to achieve pandemonium and terror then they'd succeeded, but in doing so they'd created a situation where the islander's allies had been forced to act immediately. This reeked of fools' work, Ben thought grimly, and a hostage situation, negotiating with fools was a nightmare.

Where the hell was Lily?

The question became a mantra, running through his head over and over. He asked everywhere. The islanders all knew her, but everywhere he asked he received headshakes.

'Her boy is missing and also her man. We saw her earlier but she's no longer here.'

He rounded the last corner to the roadblock before the compound. Here were the men and women he worked with, stopping anyone fool enough to risk their lives by trying to get nearer. There was someone in their midst, a woman, her voice raised.

'I know some were hurt. Let me ask. I'm a doctor. They'll let me in. Please, please, I beg you…'

Lily.

And he knew his colleagues' answer before he heard it. First rule of hostage situations—damage limitation. However many were in there, don't make it worse by sending more.

He saw Lily's shoulders slump. There was little light out here—all lights had been ordered off—and she was just a dark shadow in the moonlight. But he knew it was Lily.

She was still in theatre garb.

She looked like Lily.

'Lily,' he said, and she looked up and saw who it was. He saw the flash of recognition, but he also saw the defeat, despair and exhaustion.

'Lily,' he said again, and reached her and held her, and it was just as well.

'Ben,' she whispered, and crumpled where she stood.

He carried her back to the hospital. She'd gone past protesting; she'd gone past anything but lying limply in his arms.

What had happened to his vision of Lily as a fat mama with a brood of happy children? he asked himself. She was thinner even than he remembered. She was only five feet four, a woman of half French parentage, and that parentage showed. She'd stood out from every other medical student in their course, looking elegant and somehow right whatever she wore.

He gazed down at her now as they approached the hospital. Here, well out of range of the hostage-takers, lights were permitted on the roads and he could clearly see her features.

Her jet-black curls were still cut into that elfin style he'd loved, tendrils clinging to her face, making her Audrey Hepburn type features seem even lovelier than he remembered. But this was a new Lily, a battered Lily. There was nothing elegant about the bloodstained jeans and T-shirt and theatre over-gown she was wearing. Dark smudges marred her lovely eyes. There was a scratch across her cheek and she'd bled a little. She looked like…like…

Lily.

Why had he let her go?

That was a dumb question. There had never been any thought of staying together, he remembered. They each had their own path in life and they hadn't coincided.

'Ben,' she managed, rousing a little as he reached the entrance to the field hospital. He kicked aside a canvas barrier and found a stretcher-bed. He set her down and her eyes widened as if she'd suddenly remembered she had to do something. 'I can't,' she whispered.

'You can,' he said. 'You have to rest. It's OK.'

'It's not OK.' She tried to sit up, and as he gently guided her back on the pillows she shoved her hands against his chest and pushed. 'I need to—'

'You need to sleep, Lily,' he said firmly. 'You've worked for thirty-six hours or more without a rest. You're exhausted past the point of collapse.'

'I must.'

'You can't.'

'Then will you do it for me?' she said wildly. 'Please… Find…Ben.'

He'd thought she'd been talking about her son. What was she talking about now? 'I'm here,' he said, but she was staring straight through him.

'Please.'

'I'll look for your son,' he told her, figuring she was verging on the delirious. 'I'll have the men start a search. Tell me about him. How old is he?'

She was focusing on the point where the canvas had been

pulled aside to form a door, as if she was expecting any minute that someone would appear.

'He'll be with Jacques. He must be.'

'Jacques?'

'Benjy,' she whispered, and the effort she'd made was too much and it was too much effort to hold her eyes open a moment longer. 'My Ben. He's six years old,' she said, defeated. 'He's six years old and he looks like you. His name's Benjy. I called him after his father.'

She slept. Just like that she faded, sinking into a sleep that was almost unconsciousness. Ben stared down at her, incredulous, questions crowding his mind.

The silence stretched out. He stared at Lily as if staring could elicit information, but of course it couldn't, and the longer he stared the more questions formed.

A six-year-old boy called Benjy...

Could it be?

No. They'd always been careful. They had been medical students, not a pair of uninformed teenagers.

She hadn't meant it. He said that to himself, thinking there were more Bens than him in the world. She could have been referring to anyone.

He thought suddenly of the last time he'd seen Lily, seven years back. He'd been excited about the life ahead of him, and he'd thought she'd been just as excited about returning here. But at the last moment she'd clung and wept and then closed her eyes and pushed him away. There'd been half an hour until her flight. But...

'Go now,' she'd whispered. 'Go.'

'Lily—'

'I can't bear it. If you stay I'll break. Please. Go.'

And suddenly, finally, he knew in his heart that what he was thinking was right. Somewhere in the chaos outside, in the dark and frightening rainforest or worse, in the midst of the hostage situation, was a little boy who was his son.

I called him after his father.

He felt…ill.

There was nothing more for him to do here. Dazed, he made his way back through the triage station to the entrance to the island's permanent hospital. Sam was sitting out on the steps, smoking.

'That'll kill you,' Ben said, but he said it almost automatically, with no passion behind it, and Sam took a couple of drags on his cigarette and ground it out under his heel.

'Don't I know it. But seeing I only smoke when I lose a patient, I'm not likely to die any time soon. Damn, the kid had been left too long.'

'Another kid?' Ben said, and his heart missed a beat. 'Who…?' It was suddenly hard to ask the question but it had to be asked. 'Not a six-year-old boy called Benjy?'

When Sam shook his head his heart started again but only just.

'A ten-year-old girl called Sophia,' Sam said. 'Head injury. She was hit with shrapnel. We drilled a burrhole to try and alleviate pressure but she died under our hands.' He shifted his foot and stared at his stubbed-out cigarette as if he regretted extinguishing it. 'What were these bastards thinking?' he exploded. 'This isn't like any sort of military coup I've ever seen. They shot anything that moved. Kids, women… I've even seen a couple of shot dogs.'

'They're mad,' Ben agreed.

'I don't like our chances of negotiating,' Sam said morosely. 'God help the hostages.'

'No.' Ben hesitated and then sat down on the step beside Sam. Sam cast him a look that was suddenly concerned and moved aside to give him room.

'Do we know how many are being held hostage?' Sam

asked, and Ben shook his head. He was trying to think straight and it wasn't working.

I called him after his father.

'I need to get a search party together,' he said and rose.

Sam rose with him. 'There are search parties from one end of the island to the other,' Sam reminded him. 'Looking for injured islanders and rounding up anyone remotely connected to a gun. Why do you need another? Are you still looking for Lily?'

'I found her,' he said. 'Her son's missing. She's just passed out on me—she's been operating for thirty-six hours straight and she's closer to being unconscious than asleep. I promised I'd look for the kid.'

'A littlie?' Sam asked, concerned, and Ben took a deep breath, knowing it had to be said. Knowing it had to be acknowledged.

'A six-year-old boy,' he managed, and took a deep breath to give him strength to say the next few words. 'A six-year-old boy called Benjy. Lily named him after his father.'

The next few hours passed in a blur. At headquarters the officers listened to Ben's story—the local doctor's son was missing, as was her fiancé—a man called Jacques—and they consulted lists.

'We're searching for them already,' the captain told him. 'Others have reported them missing. Jacques is the island's financial administrator. His bungalow's in the compound and he hasn't been seen since the uprising. He's either a hostage or dead. And Dr Lily told us about the little boy. He was sent to the beach at the first sign of trouble but he would have found his great-aunt dead and everyone gone. Maybe he was forcibly taken to the compound. Or more likely…' He didn't need to complete the sentence. 'I've pulled the searchers back now. We'll search again in the morning.'

'Why not now?'

'You know why,' the captain said patiently. 'There might still be armed men in hiding, and I'll not risk our team being picked off. If I knew for sure the kid was there and alive then I'd risk it, but I know no such thing and neither do you.' His voice softened. 'Hell, Ben, you know the rules. Is this doctor putting pressure on you?'

'She's an old friend,' Ben said heavily. 'And she's been a hero here. In the last two days she's performed medicine that'd put us to shame.'

'We'll comb the forest again at first light,' the captain promised. 'I'll double the contingent to that area. I can't promise more than that.'

'And the hostage situation?'

'There's no communication,' the captain said grimly. 'So we sit and wait for them to make the first move. The last thing we need is another bloodbath.'

'There's nothing anyone can do?'

'For the moment I'm guessing the best thing for you to do is get some sleep,' the captain said, studying his friend's face and seeing a strain there he'd never seen before. 'Hell, Ben, it's not like you to get personally involved.'

'It's not, is it?' Ben said.

'Go to bed,' the captain said, roughly concerned. 'If there's any news, I'll let you know.'

'Thanks.'

'And, Ben?'

'Yeah?'

'This lady doctor…'

'Mmm?'

'How well did you know her?' And there was suddenly a hint of an understanding smile behind the captain's bland enquiry.

But Ben didn't feel like smiling. 'I knew her well enough. But I'm going to bed,' he muttered. 'Just keep the lid on the hostage situation. That's all I ask.'

CHAPTER THREE

BEN woke at dawn, and five minutes later he was striding into the original hospital, looking for Lily.

For she was gone. The first thing he'd done had been to check her stretcher-bed and the sight of its neatly folded blanket had made him feel ill.

Hell, he'd slept six hours and he'd needed that sleep. She'd had little more than that and she'd had a lot more to catch up on.

'Where's Dr Lily?' he snapped at the first person he saw. It was Pieter. The big nurse assessed Ben's face and nodded, as if he now understood something that had been worrying him.

'You'll be Dr Ben Blayden?'

'Yes.'

'I should have realised yesterday,' the nurse told him. 'I'm afraid I wasn't thinking.'

'You should have realised what?'

'That you're our Lily's Ben. That you're our Benjy's father.'

It took the wind out of Ben's lungs, so much so that he felt as if he'd been punched. After seven years...

'Where is she?' he managed, and Pieter shook his head, troubled.

'She came in here about four a.m. I wasn't here. One of your men said she should go back to sleep but I doubt she followed instructions. Her son is missing.' Pieter's voice softened. 'If I'm not mistaken, your son is missing.'

Ben flinched. He stood, stunned, letting the words sink in.

Last night there'd been room for doubt. Lily's words had been almost incoherent, the desperate words of a woman who'd gone past the point of sense. But now… 'She's told you about me?'

'She told me that Benjy was the son of a man she met at medical school. That you'd elected to be an emergency doctor with the SAS. That she'd chosen to come home, to raise your son alone because your worlds could never meet. And then yesterday…while Lily was scouring the island she went to my wife. She sobbed to her that you were here and how could she tell you about a son when she didn't know if he was alive?'

'She never told me,' Ben whispered, trying to rid himself of this sense of unreality, not sure whether he was angry or confused or just…bereft. He should be angry, he thought. The appropriate emotion should definitely be anger, but bereft was winning.

He had a son.

Where the hell was he?

'She'd only just learned she was pregnant when she came home,' Pieter was saying, watching his face. 'This island is a very easy place to raise a child without a father. In a sense we're a huge family where parenting is done by all. She wouldn't have seen the need…'

He had it now. Anger in spades, sweeping through him with a ferocity he found breathtaking.

'She wouldn't have seen the need to tell me? She didn't think I had the right to know?'

'She said you feared relationships,' Pieter said, 'But she also said you were a moral man who'd want to do the right thing by your son. She said her decision was not to load you with that responsibility.'

'But even you know…'

'Lily and I have worked side by side for almost seven years,' Pieter said, reassuringly, as if Ben was a little unhinged and he had to settle him. Which maybe wasn't far from the truth. 'I'm the cousin of her mother. There's little about Lily I don't know.'

'So she told you and she didn't tell me.'

'I believe she thought you wouldn't want to know.' Pieter looked grave. 'This is a conversation you should be having with Lily, but this is maybe not the time for considering feelings. Lily's in desperate trouble. She needs all the help she can get.'

'Where is she now?'

The big man's face clouded. 'I don't know. Maybe that's why I'm telling you this. I should be out looking for her. She should be here helping with our wounded. As I need to be. There are shoulds everywhere.'

'There's been no word about the hostages?'

'No.'

'And this Jacques?'

'He will be fine, that one,' Pieter said, and his expression grew even more grim. 'He must be a hostage but if he is…maybe he'll be the first one to talk his way out. He is not an islander, you understand. Jacques came here when the oil was found. He helps us with our administration.'

'You don't like him?'

'He's not one of us.'

And there it was, Ben thought grimly. The reason Lily had said she could never leave the island. The islanders were family.

But even though Jacques was an outsider, Lily had agreed to marry him. He must have something.

If I'd come to her island maybe she would have married me, he thought suddenly, but it was a dumb thought. He'd never have wanted to come here, and he had a lot more to think about right now than a seven-year-old romance that had gone astray.

'Ben,' a voice called from the end of the corridor, and it was Sam, wearing theatre gear again.

'Yes?'

'They've released three of the hostages,' he said. 'Or at least they opened the front doors and shoved them out. Each of them has gunshot wounds. We need all hands in Theatre and that means you.'

Which meant another six hours operating. Six hours where they somehow managed to stabilise the injured islanders.

'But things have settled,' Ben was told by the sergeant in charge when, with surgery completed, he'd made his way to temporary headquarters. 'We've done a comprehensive sweep of the island. There are no more injured.'

'Have you seen the island doctor?'

'Lily,' the sergeant said. 'Yes. She's working in the original hospital. She knows you guys are thorough, but most of the families want to talk to her.' He hesitated. 'They've had a succession of English teachers on the island and English is spoken by everyone. But maybe if my kin had been shot I'd want my family doctor to talk me through it.'

Damn. Ben had just come from the field hospital which was next door to the original building. He turned to leave but then he remembered. It wasn't just Lily he was concerned about.

'The hostage situation?'

'We're negotiating,' the sergeant told him. 'They want transport out of here.'

'Do we know who's in there?'

'Ten islanders. The most badly injured they've tossed out. Ten fits with the number of islanders who remain missing. We don't know how many rebels.'

'Is Lily's son there?'

'Yes,' the sergeant said, and Ben felt suddenly light-headed.

'We know he's alive?' he demanded.

'One of the injured men saw him. Yes.'

'And you've told Lily?'

'She was here when we heard. She'd been everywhere on the island, checking with each search team as they came in, checking herself. We were almost as glad as she was when we heard the kid was alive.'

'And…Jacques someone?' he ventured, and there was a nod.

'We assume so. He wasn't seen by the guy we talked to but he said he heard him talking.'

'So they're both safe. And you'll negotiate transport in exchange for the hostages?'

'We don't know yet,' the sergeant said. 'These guys are dangerous. We need to get permission from higher up the line. Our politicians are talking to the only people here who are fit to speak. That's the deputy head of council and the finance councillor, and they're both still in a state of shock. But the decision to negotiate isn't up to us.'

'It has to be.'

'You want to storm the place?'

'No, but…'

'Then…' The sergeant was watching him curiously, sensing his tension. This was the team sent in as a front line at every crisis, and he knew Ben well. Ben usually worked efficiently, with little emotion. He was emotional now.

He couldn't stop being emotional.

'I need to talk to Lily.'

'We need your written assessment by dusk,' the sergeant said mildly.

'You'll have it. But the priority is Lily.'

He found her sitting outside the hospital, under a group of palms in the hospital gardens. There were three islanders with her—

an old woman and two children. The old woman was keening her distress while the children looked on in incomprehension. Ben hesitated, but then he walked close enough to listen.

Lily glanced up as he approached. He gave a slight shake of his head. The hope that had flared in her eyes faded, and she turned again to the old woman, pulling her into her arms and hugging her close.

'Hush. Kira died instantly, Mary. You know that.'

'My only sister.'

Lily didn't speak again. She simply held her, not hurrying, waiting until the woman had sobbed the worst of her grief out, waiting until she raised her head of her own accord, waiting until she was ready to talk.

'Do you want help to look after the children?' she asked her at last. 'I can find someone if you need to be alone.'

The old woman glared and pulled away as if Lily had said something obscene. She put out her arms and the children, a girl of about five and a boy of about three, scooted in and were hugged tight.

'They'll stay with me until their mother is well enough to care for them again. Or until their father can get here.'

'Here's Dr Blayden. He's here to help me with the injuries. He helped operate on your mother last night, kids. He's a hero, right when we need him.'

The kids looked up at him, doubtful, looking for a real-life hero. Ben smiled and crossed to the little group, squatting down beside them and delving in his pocket for sweets. He carried them everywhere, for just such an emergency as this.

'Tell me your names,' he said, folding the sweets into their hands before they had a chance to draw back.

'Nicki,' the little girl whispered, staring down at her lolly, while the boy huddled behind his grandmother, keeping his hand closed over the precious sweet. 'And my brother is Lanie.'

'Is your mother's name Louie?'

'Yes.'

'I did help fix her last night,' he told them.

'Nicki and Lanie were with their mother when the men came,' Lily said briefly, and Ben thought Lily knew what she was doing. Traumatised kids had to talk about what happened. 'Louie ran with them. She ran to her mother's.'

The bullet had pierced Louie's shoulder as she'd run. Ben winced. What sort of criminals shot at a mother, fleeing with her children?

'I think these men are very, very bad and very, very stupid,' he told the children. 'But our soldiers have them all in one place now and they can't hurt anyone. And your mother is getting better. You can visit her now if you like.'

'I was just coming to tell them that,' Lily said.

'She'll feel much better after she's seen you,' Ben said, and he smiled at the old lady. 'And after she's seen her mother.' He delved back into his pocket and brought out six more sweets. They were sold as Traffic Lights, round, flat shining discs, red, green and yellow. 'Choose one more each,' he told the children. 'And then I want you to choose two each to take to your mother. Can you do that?'

The children nodded and the old lady stood. Her face had cleared a little, some of the horror fading.

'My daughter truly will be well?'

'She truly will be well,' Ben said, and he and Lily stood and watched as the little family bade them farewell and went to do their hospital visiting.

Ben was left with Lily.

She looked a thousand per cent better than the night before, he thought. She'd showered and changed. She was wearing a tiny denim skirt, a T-shirt and leather sandals—hardly the attire of a doctor about to do her rounds—but he could see nothing amiss with it. Except that her legs were covered with scratches. A couple of them were deep and nasty.

'Let me see to your legs,' he said, and she gazed down as if wondering what he was talking about. Seeing the bloody scratches, she merely shrugged.

'They'll be fine. Trivial stuff.'

'Not so trivial if they get infected.'

'I have more to worry about than infected legs.'

'Maybe,' he said. 'But legs come first. You want to come voluntarily or do you want to be carried? I'm a lieutenant, you know. I have authority in this place.'

She managed a feeble smile. 'I'd rather be bribed with sweets,' she said, and he shoved a hand in his pocket and produced a handful.

'Eat one,' he said, and she shook her head.

'When did you last eat?'

'I can't remember.'

'Then eat a sweet,' he told her. 'I'll bathe those legs and then you're going to be fed.'

'But—'

'Don't argue, Dr Cyprano. As of last night your deputy head of council gave us authority in this place. I'm therefore representing the occupying force and what I say goes. You eat.'

She opened her mouth to protest. He'd been unwrapping a sweet while he'd talked and he popped it in.

'No protests.'

'No, sir,' she told him with a mouth full of red sweet. 'Or, yes, sir. I don't know which.'

He dressed her legs. She stayed silent throughout, which suited his mood. There were things that had to be said but he didn't know where to start. Bathing her scratches, applying antiseptic and dressing the worst of them gave him time to think. It was as if he was getting used to her all over again.

She lay passively on an examination trolley while he worked. She stared straight ahead, seemingly oblivious when he had to scrub, though he must have hurt her. Then he took her to the mess tent, waved away anyone who would have talked to them, sat her down and watched as she mechanically ate the pasta he brought her, as she drank coffee, and as she pushed her mug away and rose and said, 'Thank you very much, I need to go now.'

'I'm coming with you.'

Unless there were new developments Ben wasn't needed now in the hospital. The uprising had been quelled so fast that maybe they could have managed with less manpower. But the fact that they'd come fast and hard had maybe averted a greater tragedy, he thought.

But for now there were enough medics to cope with medical needs. There was no more organisation for Ben to do. He could stay by Lily's side. For she intended to go back to the roadblock in front of the compound. He knew that without asking. That was where negotiations were taking place. If he had been Lily, that was where he'd want to be.

And it was where he wanted to be. For it was his son held hostage. The concept was so overpowering he didn't know what to do with it, but all he knew was that he needed to go with her.

The roadblock was half a mile from the hospital, across the beach road. It was mid-afternoon and the heat was getting to him. Lily was lightly dressed but Ben was wearing fatigues, and he was feeling it.

'Walk on the beach,' he suggested, and Lily diverted her footsteps without saying a word.

Her silence was starting to scare him. This wasn't the Lily he remembered. She'd been bright, bubbly, fun and startlingly intelligent. Her professors had described her as smart as paint, and more than one had said it was a shame she wasn't staying in Australia to specialise. But Australia's loss would be Kapua's gain. They had all known that, and she'd never questioned her destiny.

He hadn't questioned her destiny either.

'Lily, we need to talk,' he said as they walked through the fringe of coconut palms to the beach beyond.

'What good is talking?' she whispered dully, and he heard how close to breaking point she really was.

'He'll be fine, Lily,' he said softly. 'The men and women doing the negotiating are the best. We flew them in as soon as we realised how serious the hostage situation was. They're never going to blast their way in. I've watched these people before and seen the way they work. They have all the patience in the world. It might take days but they'll get them out alive. They know their stuff.'

But Lily had only heard the one word. 'Days,' she choked. 'With those murderers? He's six years old. What he must be thinking... I should have taken him to Kira's myself. But the woman I was treating...she'd have bled to death. I couldn't. Dear God, I couldn't.'

'You had medical imperatives,' he said gently. He'd talked to the finance councillor by now—the woman was recovering in hospital—and he'd seen the wound Lily had somehow pulled together. Lily was right. If she'd taken the time to take care of her son before she'd treated her, the woman would be dead. 'You saved her life, Lily.'

'But I should have kept Benjy with me,' she whispered. 'He's my son. I'm all he has.'

'Doesn't he have Jacques?' he asked, and she looked blindly up at him, uncomprehending. 'Your fiancé's in there as well, isn't he?'

She steadied a little at that. 'Jacques,' she said, and then more strongly, 'Jacques. Maybe that's why he's there. Maybe he went to Jacques.' But then she shook her head. 'But he'd have had to come past the hospital to reach Jacques.'

'Jacques is in administration?'

'He's in charge of finance,' she told him. 'Oh, we have a finance councillor but Louise isn't exactly smart. She does what Jacques says. Except for selling oil. Louise dug her heels in over that. So did we all.' She fell silent. She was trembling, Ben saw, even though the day was hot. She was walking in the damp sand near the water's edge. Here the water was a tur-quoise blue, clear to the bottom. Ben could see fish feeding on weed drifting in and out in the shallows. The beach was wide and golden. This place was indeed a tropical paradise. That such tragedy had come to it…

Lily must have been thinking the same. A tremor ran though her, and Ben took her hand.

'He'll be OK, Lily.'

'I'm sorry,' she whispered.

'There's no—'

'I mean I'm sorry I didn't tell you about Benjy.'

He didn't answer. He couldn't.

'He's such a…such a…' She took a deep breath. 'He's very much like you. Ben, if anything happens to him and you haven't met him…' She hiccuped on a sob and then seemed to regroup. 'I thought I had the right,' she told him. 'I thought… It was me who was pregnant, not you, and I knew you'd be appalled. But seeing you here… He's your son, Ben, and I should have made the effort. Even if you didn't want him.'

'Why would I not want him?'

'What were we, Ben?' she demanded, suddenly angry. 'Babies ourselves. We were young for med school. We were young for life. You were so lit up about joining the army. You were off to save the world. Armies are used for peacekeeping, you told me, but it was excitement that was in your heart. Action. Drama. Sure, you didn't want to fight, but you did want to go wherever there was action. And me…all I wanted to do was come home. My mother had sold everything she owned to send me to med school, and the islanders helped because everyone here needed a doctor. I was as excited as you were—but I was excited at coming home to help my people.'

'Did it work out?' he asked, and she took a deep breath. There wasn't a trace of colour on her face. She looked sick.

'I guess it did,' she said slowly. 'But there was a cost. My mother died just after I got back. She had cancer. She'd known for two years but she hadn't told me because she hadn't wanted to interrupt my studies.'

'Oh, Lily…'

'You see, when I found I was pregnant I was just as shocked as you would have been. We were so careful but, then, our lecturers used to say the only sure-fire contraception is a brick wall. We're proof of that. So what could I do? You'd made it clear you never wanted a family. I couldn't burden you with one, against your wishes.' She steadied then, forcing her voice to sound neutral. 'I had to come home. As it is, I've made a life for both of us here. Every islander loves Benjy. Every islander is his uncle or his aunt or his cousin, by traditional ties if not by blood.'

'And he has Jacques?'

'He has Jacques,' she agreed, though it took her time to respond. Her voice was uncertain now, as if he'd touched a nerve.

'They don't get on?'

'Why would you ask me that?'

'It is my business if he's my son.'

'He's not your son. I won't burden you with him. He's—'

'Lily, I want him to be my son.' The words surprised them both. They stopped, and a wave, higher than usual, washed in over their feet. Lily's sandalled toes were washed clean. Ben was wearing tough army boots. The water receded and they hardly looked damp.

It was dumb to be looking at boots, Ben thought. The whole thing was dumb. Maybe Lily was right. Maybe he should back off right now.

But he had a son. By Lily.

And she looked distraught.

He reached out and touched her face. There was a fine coat of dust over everything, courtesy of setting up the field hospital on land where the grass had withered during the dry season. Dust was on Lily's face, streaked now by tears, and he tracked a tear with his finger.

I wonder what this place is like in the rainy season, he thought inconsequentially.

Lily didn't move. She submitted to his touch without comment.

'I think I loved you, Lily,' he said, and she managed a ghost of a smile.

'Benjy was conceived in love,' she whispered. 'I've always believed that.'

'It's the truth.'

'Just lucky we're older, eh?' she said, but her voice was strained to breaking point. She brushed his hand from her face, turned determinedly northward again and started walking. 'Just lucky we've found sense.'

'And you've found Jacques.'

'As you say. Do you have anyone?'

'No.'

'You're still running from relationships?'

'I don't run.'

'No.' She hesitated, and then glanced sideways at him. Cautious. 'You're angry?'

'Maybe I am.'

'Because I didn't tell you about Benjy?

'Yeah. But maybe you're right,' he said bleakly. 'Maybe seven years ago I wouldn't have wanted to know. I was dumb.'

'We were both dumb.'

'Mmm.' He kicked some more sand and tried to think of other things besides how close this woman was, and how bereft she looked, and how he wanted to…

He couldn't want. She had a life here and a son and a fiancé and he was here with a job to do.

He should be working. He should go back to the hospital and organise paperwork for the evacuations. He could help treat the minor wounds of islanders still cautiously presenting.

His team were doing that. He wouldn't be needed again unless there was a blast-out in the hostage situation.

A blast-out. Benjy. His son.

Think of something else, he thought fiercely. They were nearing the headland where the compound lay and the strain on Lily's face was well nigh unbearable. She was staring ahead as if she was willing herself to see through walls. He had to distract her.

'Lily, there's a couple of things bothering me.'

'I don't have time to—'

'Not about us,' he said gently. 'About this situation. Can you help?'

She took a deep breath and steadied. 'Of course.'

'You told me seven years ago that this island was like a huge family. Everyone knew everyone and no one locked their doors. Is that right?'

'Yes, but—'

'But what?' he asked. 'The insurgents were forced to leave the hospital alone, and we've been wondering why. We've been told there's been a drug problem on the island, so you've trained orderlies to act as security guards. Is that right?'

'Yes, but—'

'Do you know these drug users? Are they locals?'

'No,' she said slowly, and he knew she was having trouble concentrating, but she was determined to try. 'We've had three break-ins over the last two months. None before. Down south there's a surf camp. The surf here is fantastic and devotees come to train, but for the last couple of months there's been guys there who are worrying. They just lie around and drink, and the break-ins started at the same time they arrived. They've had three-month visas. Our local policeman couldn't find evidence to deport them, so he trained and armed our orderlies and we let it be known.' She gave a rueful smile. 'Our orderlies are the most peaceable of men, but it acted like a deterrent. The break-ins stopped.'

'So where are these men now?'

'Maybe I heard they were to go to one of the outer islands. I'm not sure.'

'You never thought to get a profile on any of them?'

'I'm a doctor. I didn't think anything.'

'But you—'

'It's not my responsibility,' she flashed. 'Ben, if you knew how hard I work... There's no other doctor on any of these islands. Kapua's the biggest in the chain but there's twenty inhabited islands. The health service is me. No one wants to fly to Australia for treatment. Hardly anyone will leave their own island. Pregnant mothers are supposed to fly out to Fiji to give birth but hardly any do. Elderly islanders won't leave, no matter how sick they are. I fly by the seat of my pants, doing what comes next, and policing isn't on my list. Sure, our policeman should have investigated more, and maybe if I'd thought of it I would have reminded him, but I didn't. I was just grateful the break-ins stopped.'

'I'm sorry,' he said, startled by her anger, and she stooped and picked up a shell and tossed it into the sea with such savagery that she came very near to knocking out a seagull. The gull rose with a startled shriek and Lily stared at it for a moment and then sighed.

'Sorry, bird,' she said. And then, 'Sorry, Ben. It's just… during med school everyone—including you—assumed I was coming home to an idyllic island existence. But this place… We need a full medical service, with helicopter evacuation, with at least two doctors and a set-up where I can do operations that involve more than me cutting frantically while I'm instructing Pieter in the niceties of anaesthesia.' She broke off, turned her face to the council compound again and winced.

He tugged her against him. For a moment she resisted, staying rigid in his grasp, but he on kept holding her, willing some of his strength into her.

'I promise we'll keep your son safe,' he said softly. 'I swear.'

But what sort of dumb promise was that? How could he make it good?

But she finally gave in and let herself lean against him. His arms held her and he smelt the citrus fragrance of her hair. Memories flooded back of the Lily of seven years ago and he thought, She's the same Lily, my Lily. And with that thought came self-knowledge. If there was a choice… If he could walk into the compound and say let the boy go, take him instead, he'd do just that.

For Lily.

But it wasn't just for Lily. For things had changed. The child in the compound wasn't just Lily's son. He was his own son.

He had family.

The thought was incredible. His world had changed, he thought, dazed. It had shifted on its axis, leaving everything he knew unaligned.

And suddenly, desperately, he wanted to kiss this woman,

properly, as she needed to be kissed, as he ached to kiss her, taking her lips against his mouth, possessing the sweet core of her. Loving her…

But he knew that if he did that, she'd pull back. She was terrified for her son. She was taking strength from him and he wanted her to keep doing that. So hold yourself back, he told himself fiercely, though God only knew what effort that cost him.

But somehow he managed it, kissing her hair, but lightly, as one would have comforted a distressed child. He stood, holding her as she leaned against him. Warmth flowed between them. It was as if she was admitting finally that she needed help; she needed him.

But with that thought came an answering one. He needed her. Lily.

He couldn't pull her tighter into him. He mustn't. What was happening here was too precious to be destroyed by stupid impulses, no matter how strong those impulses might be.

'Let's go,' he said gently, and somehow he put her away from him and smiled gently down into her strained-to-exhaustion face. 'Let's go and find our son.'

'Of course,' she said dully. 'If we can.'

'We will,' he said. 'We'll do this together. We're together until we find him.'

'Ben…'

He pulled her against him once more, but gently, as one would have comforted a friend. She was his friend. She was the mother of his child. He hugged her and then he linked his hand in hers and led her forward.

'You're not alone, Lily,' he told her. 'I'll be here for you for however long it takes.'

CHAPTER FOUR

THE days wore on, and the nights. Each night Ben lay in the dark and listened to the soft breathing of the woman in his arms. Imperceptibly his world changed.

Lily needed him, in a way he'd never been needed in his life.

This crisis didn't stop medical imperatives occurring elsewhere, and Lily had refused to stop working as the island's doctor. Ben and his team tried to take as much of the load from her as they could but the islanders made no secret of the fact that they trusted only Dr Lily.

'Just refuse to go,' Ben told her.

'I'll go crazy with nothing to do,' she'd say. 'Besides, there's a girl in labour on an outer island.' Or… 'There's an old man in severe pain. This is my normal workload, Ben. The islanders trust me but no one else. You're an outsider.'

He was an outsider, but he wasn't an outsider to Lily. He was father to an island child. A child he'd never met. The situation was surreal.

How Lily could work…

She could work only because she had him. He knew that by now, and so did everyone on the island. At the end of a long day she'd drag herself back to her bungalow behind the hospital and he'd make sure he was there waiting for her. She'd fall into his arms, exhausted with the fears and the frustrations and the pain of a day filled with medical need. He'd hug her close but carefully, rigidly—he'd take it no further. He mustn't. She'd run and she mustn't run. So he'd hold her and he'd tell her what, if anything, had changed in the hostage situation. Sometimes she'd cry and if she did he'd let her cry her fill. Then he'd cradle her to sleep as he'd cradled her tonight.

Seven years ago he'd lain with Lily as a man lay with the woman he loves. Their loving then had been exciting and fun and happy.

This time there was no love-making—or love-making in the sexual sense. She had no energy left for sex, and his desire for her had changed. He wanted her to sleep. He wanted her to drift into an unconsciousness where she didn't have to be ter-rified for her son.

This was a different sort of love-making, he thought. The girl he'd loved was gone. What was left was the mother of his son.

He loved her?

No, he told himself. In truth he didn't really understand it himself. He only knew that if the choice was an exciting return to the love-making of old or achieving a measure of peace for the woman he held in his arms, the choice was a no-brainer.

He hardly slept himself. That was no problem—he'd learned to exist on catnaps. He could survive. But the nights stretched on and he held on. He held his woman and his world…changed.

'I shouldn't be letting you do this,' Lily whispered to him in the dark. 'It's not fair.'

'I need this, too,' he told her. 'It's our son, Lily. Let's do this together.'

The end, when it came, was swift and deadly.

It was three in the morning. Lily was sleeping fitfully, nestled against him, her breasts moulded to his chest with only the flimsy fabric of her sleepwear between them. He'd been cradling her in his arms, murmuring softly to her at need, re-assuring her when she'd wake at every unexpected noise.

And then he heard it. A low murmur at first, then building until it was a cacophony of sound heading towards them.

Helicopters. Big ones. He was out of bed, hauling on his pants and groping for his boots as Lily jerked into terrified wakefulness.

'What is it?'

'Choppers,' he said, his fingers clumsy in his haste. 'Not ours. Hell. We knew they had to have outside help. Lily, stay here.'

'In your dreams. Benjy—'

'I'll take care of him,' he said, and set his hands on her shoulders and propelled her back on the pillows. 'I swear I'll take care of him. Lily, please. Stay here.'

'I can't.'

'If you won't stay, I can't go,' he said. The helicopters were almost overhead and he knew what they'd be aiming for. But did they come with death to the islanders in mind? Surely not. 'Lily, promise me. Stay here until I bring Benjy to you.'

'I—'

'You must.' He had to go. There was no time to wait for promises. He kissed her, hard and fast and strong, taking strength from her as well as giving it. He grabbed the torch he'd left at the door, and he was gone.

Ben ran toward the compound. There were four helicopters— no, five—hovering overhead.

The moon was a mere sliver, its rays hardly reaching through the clouds. It had been steamy all day, and tonight it had rained. Maybe that's why they'd come tonight, he thought as he ran, keeping to the cover of the trees.

Why were they there?

And then the clouds parted for a moment and he topped a slight rise and saw.

The compound backed onto the beach. Despite the dim light, Ben could suddenly see the whole picture. While four choppers hovered, one helicopter was behind, protected, and it was landing on the beach.

Ben stood stock still. His job was to stay in the background and wait for casualties, assessing medical need, so he had to stay back now. Troops were running past, keeping to the shadows.

But the hostages…

A message rang out loudly. The sound system had been set up initially as a tsunami warning—a long, low siren—but technicians had tweaked it a couple of days ago, making it capable of transmitting voices, so in an emergency all could be warned of anything at all.

Now the warning was urgent. 'Take cover,' a voice boomed and Ben recognised their bass-voiced drill sergeant. 'Don't take aggressive action. I repeat, take cover.'

'Thank you,' Ben breathed, as he forced himself to wait some more. His team was good.

He realised now that the choppers were simply providing cover for an escape bid, giving the fifth chopper time to land and assist those leaving the compound.

He'd pulled further back into the shadows of the palms. The choppers had floodlights and they were searching the shadows.

A hand landed on his shoulder and he came as near to yelping as a grown man could.

'Ben.'

Lily! He grasped and held her. 'How the hell…? I told you to stay back.' She was dressed in windcheater and jeans—she must have moved as fast as he had.

'I can't.'

He tugged her back into the shadows, hauling her tight against him. 'How did you know where I was?'

'I followed you,' she whispered. But she wasn't concentrating on him. She was staring skyward, appalled. 'What's happening?'

'There's a chopper landing on the beach. The others are covering it. Whoever's in the compound will be going out the back way.' He grimaced and hauled her tighter.

'Why don't we stop them?'

'We could,' Ben said grimly, staring up. 'But there's four choppers directly over the compound. If we shoot, we risk a chopper coming straight down. They know that. See how they're clustered over the buildings. That's a defence in itself. Second…'

'Second?'

'We don't know who they are,' he said grimly. 'Those choppers are huge and expensive. We shoot them down, we find out who they are and we have to face the reality of maybe a neighbour being an armed aggressor. If they're here simply to get their people out of a bungled situation then our orders are to resolve a situation—not to start a conflict.'

'But Benjy,' she said wildly. 'If they take Benjy… How can you think politics when it's our child?'

Our child. The words pierced him, making him want to put away everything he'd ever been taught, making him want to run into the compound right now.

It'd help no one and he knew it. He tugged her harder against him. She was no fool, but where a child was concerned… His child…

'We have to wait,' he told her, and God only knew how hard it was to say it.

'But if they take him…'

'Why would they take him? Lily, we just have to believe they won't.'

* * *

And then it was over, as quickly as it had started. The chopper on the beach rose into the night sky to join its companions. They gathered together above the compound, a menacing, hulking threat, and then suddenly the five machines swept off together at full power, growing smaller and smaller until they disappeared.

They hadn't disappeared before Ben and Lily were running into the compound, hand in hand, stumbling through the darkness in shared terror.

Benjy....

The sound of the helicopters was still fading in the distance as Ben shone his torch into one room after another, while men shouted warnings from outside, saying not to enter until it had been checked. But neither of them were listening and Lily was clutching Ben's hand with a fierceness that urged him to move faster.

They found them. The hostages had been herded into one small bungalow at the end of the row. They were bound together, huddled against the furthest wall, their faces blank with terror.

All except one. One hostage was a child, and even as Ben swung the flashlight to find him Lily had her son in her arms, and she was holding him so tightly that it might be quite a while before anyone saw Benjy Cyprano again.

CHAPTER FIVE

MIRACULOUSLY there were no more deaths. The official decision not to oppose the rescue effort had been the saving of many, Ben thought gratefully as he worked through the night. The sound system's message and the noise of the choppers had made everyone seek refuge.

There were shock cases among the hostages, as well as gunshot wounds. The hostages were a trembling, stunned muddle of emotions, and Ben thought they'd need to bring in psychologists to counsel them.

As for Benjy... 'I'm taking him home,' Lily had said, solidly, loudly, as if she had been defying anyone to argue. Ben had been needed, so he'd reluctantly nodded to one of his men to accompany her—to see her home safely. She'd disappeared into the night and he hadn't seen her since.

Benjy was physically unharmed. For now that was all that mattered. He wanted desperately to go to them, but he couldn't.

Medical imperatives... He had a job to do.

It was almost midday the next day before he surfaced from the field hospital and could hand over the hospital to Sam.

'I'm going to Lily's,' he said, and Sam looked thoughtful.

'The whole army's relieved we got the kid out,' he said. Then he hesitated. 'You know, the islanders think the sun rises and sets around Lily. But there's talk. There's no sign of the boy-friend. It was assumed he was a hostage, but he's not.'

Ben knew that. The unknown Jacques. Lily's fiancé.

'Do you think he's an organiser?' Sam asked bluntly.

'I'm betting he is,' Ben said grimly.

'That's what we're thinking. The big boys will be wanting to talk to your Lily.'

'She's not my Lily.'

Sam raised his brows in mock enquiry. 'Not?'

'She's engaged.'

'To Jacques. Who's not here. I suspect she's not engaged any more, boyo.' He raised his brows. 'And the boy? There's rumours…'

'Scotch them.'

'Of course,' Sam said blithely, but Ben knew exactly where the rumours stemmed from and he knew there was nothing he could do about it.

He was wasting time. He had to see Lily.

Ben knocked and entered the little bungalow behind the hospital. There was no answer. He hesitated but he'd been in and out of this bungalow so many times over the last few days he felt he had the right. He pushed the door. It swung inward and he went right on in.

They were asleep.

For a moment the sight of them knocked him sideways. Lily's bedroom door was ajar. From the sitting room he could see them clearly, a woman and a child huddled together on a big bed, holding each other tightly even in sleep.

He went further in. They didn't stir.

Lily had been crying. He could see tear stains on her dusty face. The choppers, flying low, had sent up a swirl of dust and sand, and everyone who'd been near them had been coated. Lily was no exception.

She looked so young, he thought. She looked almost as young as the child in her arms.

And the boy? This was the first time he'd been able to see him clearly. Benjy.

Called after his father.

Ben stood stock still, taking in every detail. Benjy was six years old and skinny, his small face freckled and open. He was wearing stained shorts and a filthy T-shirt. His legs were bare and grubby. His small feet were callused as if his constant state was barefoot. Of course, he thought. This was an island child.

This was his child. His arms were twined around his mother's neck and his small nose was flattened against her breast.

He looked…like him.

There was a photo he had somewhere of himself at the same age, Ben thought, stunned into immobility. The likeness was unmistakable.

Benjy.

Safe with his mother.

He didn't cry. Hell, he never cried. Such a thing was unthinkable.

But the kid was…

'Ben.' With a start he realised Lily was awake. She was looking up at him with eyes that were uncertain. Almost as soon as she saw him her gaze went to her son, as if making sure his reality was not some hopeless dream. 'Ben,' she whispered again as the sleep faded from her eyes, and he wasn't sure who she was referring to.

'I'm glad he's safe.' It was inadequate but he couldn't think of anything else to say.

'Are there more casualties?'

'Five injured hostages, from the original attack, none critical. It's over, Lily.'

'They've gone?'

'Yes.'

'And…Jacques?'

'He's gone, too.'

'I see,' she whispered, and her lips touched Benjy's filthy hair. 'Do you need me?'

'No. I just came to make sure…'

'Benjy's fine. He's not hurt. He said…Jacques looked after him.'

Ben had guessed that much. However wicked Jacques was, there must have been a vestige of fondness for the boy. Otherwise he'd have been thrust out with the other rejected hostages. Or killed.

At least he hadn't taken him with him.

'I don't understand,' Lily whispered and neither did Ben. It might take weeks for this story to be pieced together, if indeed it ever could be.

'Let's leave it for now,' he said softly, and he stooped and kissed her softly on the forehead. He brushed tears from her eyes with his fingers, and then knelt and kissed her again. On the lips. She didn't move, just lay passive, not welcoming his kiss but not pushing him away either. Maybe she needed the contact as much as he did.

But he couldn't stay. Not now she had her son back. For that would be admitting something he couldn't begin to admit. A need of his own?

No.

'Just sleep,' he told her. 'We have two doctors and six para-medics on duty, and there's nothing for you to do but to care for your son.'

'Our son,' she whispered, and he felt his gut twist as he'd never felt it twist before.

'Our son,' he repeated, and he stood and stared down at them for a very long time.

Until Lily's eyes closed again.

She held her son now and not him.

He was no longer needed.

He left them. Somehow.

When she appeared at the hospital the next morning Ben told her sternly she was to spend the next few days with her son, that she wasn't to think of anything else, that he and Sam and Pieter had things under control. She looked at him blankly and left, but she didn't go home. On this island everyone knew everyone's whereabouts and Pieter told Ben what she was doing. She was working her way through the island homes, talking to each family about what had happened, and there was nothing Ben could do to stop her.

In medical school they'd been taught to stay emotionally detached. Emotional detachment on Kapua? The concept was ridiculous.

The concept of such involvement left Ben cold, but he couldn't remonstrate. He didn't understand why she needed to do this, but she did. And he had to take a back seat emotionally as well. She had enough emotional baggage already, without him adding more.

She'd need time to come to terms with Jacques's betrayal.

For it had been betrayal. It had been confirmed that Lily's fiancé had been in the group of insurgents who'd made the break away from the island.

'He was with them,' Ben had been told, and he'd had to say as much to Lily.

She hardly seemed to take it in. She desperately needed time.

So did he, he thought grimly as he worked on. How did you come to terms with fatherhood?

At least there was work enough to keep his mind busy elsewhere. Somehow the night of the hostage drama had changed the islanders' distrust of outside doctors. Whether it was Sam's big mouth or Pieter's he wasn't sure, but it was suddenly known everywhere that Ben was Benjy's father. And if he was Benjy's father then he had the right to protect Lily, to say, no, she couldn't come, her first priority had to be Benjy. Astonishingly the consensus now was that he had the right to treat the islanders.

How did Lily manage? he asked himself as the days wore on. He hadn't realised—had anyone?—what a medical centre Kapua had become. Lily was the island doctor not just for Kapua. She was island doctor for a score of smaller islands as well.

There was such need. In the three days after the hostage release he saw trauma as great as that caused by the uprising. Two men drowned on an outer island—they'd been fishing drunk and had ended up on rocks. Two boys survived the accident but they were now in hospital, one with a broken leg, one with multiple lacerations and shock. As well as that, he had viruses to deal with. He had infections. There was a manic depressive who'd refused to take her medication and was seeing aliens. There was a childbirth.

That was one where he'd really wanted Lily. The girl had gone into premature labour. The women caring for the expectant mother had rung the hospital to ask Lily to come, but they hadn't said what the need was. When they'd heard Lily wasn't available they'd simply hung up and tried to cope themselves. By the time they'd admitted defeat and called Ben, he'd had a premature baby of thirty weeks gestation on his hands.

It had still taken all his persuasive powers before mother and child had agreed to being flown to Fiji. 'Lily will fix my baby when she's back at work,' the girl had said, desperately trying to ignore the fact that her baby had major breathing difficulties. In the end Ben had simply said, 'Ruby, Lily can't help you. You go to Fiji on the next flight, or you have a dead baby.'

Ruby had conferred with the island women and had finally agreed that, yes, she and her baby could go, but there had been an unspoken undercurrent. If Lily had been there, she'd have fixed the baby herself. What did you expect of a male doctor interfering in women's business?

What Lily must have to cope with…

He ached to talk to her but he knew she had to have space. Somehow he let her be.

On the third evening he returned from an outer island late. An old lady with bone metastases had needed pain relief but she wasn't stirring from home, and it had taken him hours to get her settled and pain free. Finally, exhausted, he headed for the mess tent to face a congealed dinner. He carried his unappealing plate over to an empty table—and Lily walked in.

She was such a different Lily to the Lily he'd met and loved at med school, he thought. Oh, she was still dressed as she always was, as she had been then, in light pants and simple T-shirt. Her curls were washed and shining and her features were those of the Lily of old. She was smiling, with a trace of the laughter he remembered so well.

But the strain behind her eyes was dreadful.

She had her Benjy back, but there were still losses that must ache, he thought. Kira had been like a mother to Lily since her own mother had died. He'd gleaned that much from island gossip. Lily's grief for the old woman would be raw and deep.

There were few secrets on this island and wherever he went people talked of Lily. Even though he was taking away her load of acute medicine, he knew she was working with traumatised islanders, listening to them, being one of them, acting more effectively than any trauma counsellor his team could possibly provide.

'Hi,' she said, with that lovely trace of a French accent.

'Hi,' he said back, and attempted another mouthful of... What was this?

'I hear you've been out saving my world.' She sat and smiled across at him. 'Thank you, Ben,' she said, and his gut twisted, just like that. A simple thank you...

'I haven't saved everybody,' he said. 'I sent Ruby Mannering and her baby to Fiji. The women infer that if you'd been there no such trip would be necessary. And a couple of fishermen drowned on Lai. I know it's unlikely, but I have the distinct impression if you'd been around you could have brought them back from the dead.'

Her smile faded. 'I heard about them,' she admitted. 'Morons. And as for Ruby and the baby...' Her smile returned again, just a little. 'Sure, I would have sent her to Fiji and if I'd known she was pregnant I would have sent her earlier. But she didn't tell me she was pregnant and for once the island's grapevine let me down. I need to get over there and box some ears.'

'I can imagine you boxing ears.'

Her smile returned. 'You'd better believe it. If they want me to care for them then they have to tell me what's going on. I have enough problems without unexpected births.'

'You have enough problems anyway,' he said gently. 'This set-up is impossible.'

'It is what it is,' Ben,' she said. 'There's no point in questioning it.'

There was a moment's silence. So much to say. Ben attempted another bite of whatever lay on his plate—maybe lasagne?—and gave up. He pushed the plate aside and the mess sergeant came over to collect it.

'Not hungry?'

'No,' Ben lied. 'They fed me out on Lai.'

There was another silence. They were alone in the mess tent

now, apart from the two men behind the workbench. It was hot in there, and still.

'You want to go for a walk?' Lily suggested.

'Where's Benjy?'

'Asleep. Henri's dad, Jean, is staying at my house. Henri's getting on well, but Jean's having nightmares. Sam's sending Henri to Sydney in the next couple of days for reconstructive surgery but meanwhile Benjy and I are helping keep Jean's nightmares at bay.'

Here it was again. Lily, taking on the troubles of her world.

'But you're here,' he said, thinking she couldn't be keeping other people's nightmares at bay if she was out of the house.

'Jean's watching rugby on television,' Lily said, and that faint smile returned again. 'There are limits on neighbourliness. Come on. It's better outside and maybe we need to talk.'

So they left. It was cooler outside, the ocean breeze making the night lovely.

'Do you want to go to the beach?' he asked tentatively.

'Wait here for a minute.' She was gone for three or four minutes and when she returned she was carrying a basket. 'Dinner,' she said. 'I can see a lie when it rises up and bites me, and you saying you'd eaten on Lai was a great big lie, Dr Blayden.'

'It might have been,' he admitted cautiously, and she chuckled, a lovely, throaty chuckle that he'd almost forgotten but when he heard it again... How could he have forgotten?'

'Egg and bacon pie,' she told him. 'Sushi rolls. Chocolate éclairs.'

'You've been cooking!' He was astounded, and she chuckled once more.

'How little you know of this island. The currency here is food. I'm the islanders' doctor, therefore I have more food than I know what to do with. This week the island's cooks have been working overtime. There's not a family affected by this tragedy that doesn't have an overstocked pantry.'

'Great,' he said, because he couldn't think what else to say. He followed as she led him to the path down to the beach. There was enough light to see by, enough light for Lily to choose a spot on the sun-warmed sand, spread a rug and then plop down on her knees and unpack. As he didn't follow suit, she looked up at him.

'What?' she demanded.

And he thought, What indeed? He didn't have a clue.

The tide was far out. The sand was soft and warm and the moonlight made the setting weirdly intimate—a picnic rug in the night with this woman whom he'd known so well seven years ago but not known since.

He was still in his uniform, heavy khaki. He felt overdressed.

'You could take your boots off,' she suggested, as though she'd read his mind, and he smiled and sat and hauled his boots off, and that made it more intimate still.

'Eat,' she ordered, and that was at least something to do. Actually, it was more than something. Whoever was doing Lily's cooking knew their stuff.

'You don't need army rations while you're here,' she said. 'Help yourself to my fridge.'

'I'm not sure how much longer we'll be here.'

'Sam was saying. I talked to him today while you were away. But we have fifteen islanders still in hospital with injuries that need rehabilitation. Sam's thinking we'll have to airlift them out.'

'They'll hate it,' Ben said, who knew enough of the island mindset by now to realise such an airlift would create major problems. For patients like Henri who'd need further recon-structive surgery, the islanders would consider evacuation regret-table but reasonable. But if the patient was slowly recovering and all they needed was supervision and rehabilitation…

'I can't cope if we don't,' Lily said, and he heard a hint of despair behind the words.

'You won't have to. We'll work things out. Maybe some of our medical staff can stay.'

'Presupposing here's no crisis anywhere else in the region.'

'There is that. But, Lily—'

'You'll be wanting to talk about Jacques,' she said dully, changing the subject as if she couldn't bear talking about the last one. 'Everyone wants to talk about Jacques.'

'I don't especially.' He knew he sounded cautious. Hell, he was cautious. If she hadn't wanted to talk about evacuating the injured, how much more difficult would it be to talk about Jacques?

'I've been talking to your intelligence people,' she muttered bleakly. 'Intelligence…that's more than I have.'

He still wasn't sure where to go with this. 'Don't beat yourself up,' he tried, and she responded with anger.

'Easy for you to say. You didn't agree to marry someone who turns out to have betrayed the whole island.'

'He's a smart man, Lily. It wasn't just you he conned.'

For the essentials had been worked out by now. It must have been no accident that Jacques arrived on the island just after the council had decided not to sell their oil. Maybe they could be persuaded to change their minds. But no one had been persuaded, and Jacques's attempts to drum up political change had been met not just with apathy but with incomprehension. Then Jacques and whatever political power was behind him must have decided to take over by force. They must have thought no one would notice the distress of such a small island.

But the thugs sent to carry out the operation had been idle for too long, aching for a fight. Maybe Jacques had argued for more time, for better trained men. The hostages said that Jacques had been appalled at what had happened, knowing such bloodshed must have been bound to cause international response. But that didn't help Lily, who was staring out at the darkened sea, her face bleak and self-judging.

'You loved him?' he asked, and anger resurfaced.

'What do you think?'

'I guess you did if you agreed to marry him.'

'He was here for three years before I agreed.'

'That's a pretty long courtship.' He wasn't sure where she was taking this, but he didn't know where he was going either, so he may as well join her.

'He was great to Benjy,' she said, and some of the anger faded. 'He was smart and funny and kind. He transformed the island's financial situation. He worked so hard...'

'While he tried to persuade you to sell the oil.'

'That was the only thing we disagreed about. Six months ago, when he was given the final knock back, he just exploded, telling me the islanders were fools, they were sitting on a fortune and if they didn't want it, others did. He was just...vitriolic.'

'And then?'

'Then he just seemed to accept it,' Lily said. 'He stopped haranguing our politicians and just focused...well, on being nice again. On being...perfect.'

'So you agreed to marry him.'

'There wasn't anyone else,' she said. 'After you.'

He drew in his breath. It had to be talked about some time. It had to be now.

'Ours was a great friendship,' he said softly, and then watched as her anger returned.

'Is that how you think of it? As a friendship?'

'Don't you think that?'

'I loved you, Ben,' she snapped. 'I've never thought anything other than that. I broke my heart when we went our separate ways.'

There was a moment's silence while he thought that through.

For the life of him he couldn't think what to do with it. She'd loved him? Had he loved her? He'd been a kid, he thought, a useless kid just starting out on the adventure of life.

He hadn't known how to love a woman. He still didn't know.

'You should have told me about Benjy,' he said finally, and it sounded lame even to him.

'You wouldn't have wanted to know. You think back to what you wanted then—to be in the middle of every hot spot this world had to offer. Where did a child fit into that?'

'I would have...' He paused and she answered for him.

'What, Ben? Sent him a cheque at Christmas and a signed photo of his daddy doing brave and daring things all over the world?'

'That's not fair.'

She hesitated. For a moment he thought she was going to make some hot retort, but in the end she didn't.

'No, it's not fair,' she agreed at last. 'And you're right. I should have told you. Any number of times over the last seven years I've thought you should know, but...'

'Were you afraid I'd come?'

She shrugged. 'Maybe that was it. But I'm over it.'

She was over loving him? That was good. Wasn't it?

She'd loved Jacques.

'We're grown up now,' he agreed at last. 'We're sensible. We don't do the heart thing any more.'

'Did you ever do the heart thing?'

'Lily...'

'I know,' she whispered. 'It's not fair to ask if you loved me seven years ago. We were kids. But I did feel grown up in the way I felt about you.'

'As you felt...grown up about Jacques?'

'Even more grown up,' she said. 'And just as stupid. That was a decision of the head and look where that got me.' She rose and brushed sand from her pants, looking uncertainly back toward the hospital. 'I need to go.'

'I'd like to get to know Benjy before I leave.'

'Of course.'

It worried him, he decided, that she was being calmly courteous. This was a reasonable discussion, but he didn't feel reasonable. He felt like hitting something. 'Maybe I need to do that fast,' he told her. 'Most of the troops will be pulling out in the next few days.' Then, as he saw the flash of fear behind her eyes, he said, 'Lily, there's no need to fear anyone coming back. No one's naming names but we know who was behind this. Nothing can be said, no accusations can be made, but they'll be aware that the eyes of the world are on them now and they daren't try again. I suspect…maybe the islanders aren't as innocent as they thought you were.'

'How can we be innocent when so many of our number are dead?' she said, not attempting to hide her bitterness. 'And that they be allowed to get away with murder…' She faltered, and closed her eyes. Ben stepped forward, but her eyes flew open and she stepped away. 'Don't touch me.'

'I only—'

'I'm not the Lily you knew.'

'I can see that,' he said gravely. 'To have coped with the medical needs of this community for so long…'

'I'm fine,' she said. 'I'm fine because I have support from all the islanders. You know, when I came back here seven years ago there was a part of me that didn't want to come. But now…'

'You want to put up the barricades.'

'Jacques was an outsider and look what he caused. I should have known. So, yes, I want you all gone. I want my life normal—like it was before Jacques was here. How could I ever have been stupid enough to believe him? First you, then him. My choice of men…'

'You're putting me in the same category as Jacques?' he demanded, appalled, but no apology was forthcoming.

'Look at you,' she said scornfully. 'A grown man, chasing danger like it's some sort of adrenalin rush…'

'I don't need it.'

'Yes, you do,' she said, weariness replacing anger. 'I asked you to come and see my island when we finished med school and you know what you said? You said, "I've no intention of wasting time sleeping under coconut palms." As if my life has anything to do with sleeping. And now… You're on this island because it's what you term exciting. Someone else might stay behind and help me pick up the pieces but it won't be you. Sam told me…'

'Sam,' Ben said, and groaned inwardly, because Sam was the last person he'd want to be telling Lily what he was like now. 'What's Sam been saying?'

'Sam said you're a frontline doctor,' she said. 'You go in first. The heroic Lt Blayden. Where danger is, that's where you are.'

'So?' he said, cautious, unable to think of any way to avoid a criticism he didn't really understand.

'So maybe that's why I haven't told Benjy about you.'

'What have you told him about his father?'

'Not much,' she said, and flushed. 'Ben, this is crazy. I'm way out of my league. I've spent the last few days thinking Benjy might have been killed. That should make the rest of this discussion trivial, but it's not. It still matters.'

'I do want to get to know him.'

'So stay on,' she said, challenging. 'If a medic can stay here as long as the field hospital's needed, why can't that person be you?'

'My job means I don't stay in one place,' he said blankly.

'And my job is to protect Benjy,' she said, as if he'd ended the conversation. 'I need to get back to him.'

'I'll come with you.'

'I don't want you in my house.' She took a deep breath. 'I know. That sounds dumb—and mean. While Benjy was in danger I needed you—I needed anyone—and you sleeping in my house helped. But it doesn't help now. It only complicates things.'

'Why?'

'Because I don't need you any more,' she told him simply. 'I don't need you and I don't need Jacques. End of story. You've taught me a hard lesson, Ben Blayden, but maybe I'm finally learning. So go back to your quarters and move on.'

'And Benjy?'

'I can't figure that out. Maybe I will in the morning. I'm too tired now. It's too late at night and I'm not sleeping.'

'Lily—'

'Leave it,' she snapped. 'I don't want you being sympathetic. I don't want you to be anything at all. I just want everything to be as it was.'

'It can't be.'

'You think I don't know that?' she yelled, and her voice rose so high that a flock of native birds flew upward from the palms in sudden fright. She backed away from him, taking some of her anger out in movement. She glared at him, turned away and kicked out as the remains of a wave reached up to her toes. Water sprayed up around her, and then retreated. She was left alone on a patch of washed sand, shimmering in the moonlight.

Shimmering blue.

Electric blue.

Where a moment ago it had been dark and lifeless, suddenly a thousand lights had turned on around her feet.

She stood absolutely still and the lights slowly faded. But they were still there, a thousand, no, a million tiny blue lights shining from within the wash of white water surging in and out with the tide.

'Oh,' she whispered, deflected from her anger.

Light was everywhere. She gazed down at her feet and she wiggled her toes experimentally.

The lights went on around her.

'Oh.' It was scarcely a breath. It was a whisper of awe.

She bent and put a hand on the sand. Lifting it, she left a perfect handprint of light, shimmering blue. She stared down, awed, as the lights slowly went out again and her handprint became nothing but a darker patch in the wet sand. But still there were lights. Wherever the water washed, there was light.

'What is it?' she breathed. 'Oh, Ben…'

He was as awed as she was. But he did know what it was. He'd seen this once before, on the south coast of Australia, and it had blown him away then as it was doing again now.

'It's bioluminescence,' he told her. 'It's millions of tiny sea creatures called dinoflagellates. You rarely see them this close to shore. They're like fireflies, responding to movement with a tiny blue glow.'

'It's not magic?' She was turning round and round, very slowly, watching her feet glow around her.

'Almost.' In truth he was as awed as she was. 'Maybe it is. It surely looks magic.'

'Oh, Ben…'

He walked down the beach until he was beside her. As soon as he reached the soaked sand, his footprints lit up blue just like Lily's.

'This wasn't here when we came. We'd have noticed,' Lily breathed. 'How…?'

'They'll have come in on the tide.'

'They never have before.'

'It's rare as hen's teeth this close in.'

'It's…' She was still turning, slowly, with her hands held out, like a ballet dancer. She sank and dug her hands into the soaking sand. Lifting them high, the sand fell from her fingers in a shower of blue light.

She laughed, a laugh of pure delight, a laugh he hadn't heard for so long.

'It's magic,' she whispered. 'It's just magic.'

'It is.' He caught her as she rose and spun once more, and he tugged her against him. They stood side by side, their bodies touching, water washing over their feet, gazing out at a sea that was a wash of blue and shimmering silver, a magic show put on just for them. Just for this night.

They didn't speak. There was no need. The wonder of the night was before them—and it was also within them, Ben thought as he held her close and watched her wonder.

How could he have left this woman? She was so beautiful…

'Lily,' he said at last, uncertainly, and she took a deep breath, cast one last wondering look at the sea and then tugged away from him. Just a little, but enough.

'That was…awesome, Ben,' she managed. 'But I need to go.

'Lily—'

'Don't,' she said as he looked down at her in the moonlight, and they both knew what he meant. Don't take this further.

They were no longer lovers, he thought, and this was a night for lovers. This was a scene set for lovers.

She was right. They had to move on.

'Thank you for tonight, Ben,' she whispered, her voice suddenly ragged at the edges. She was forcing herself to break the moment. She was forcing herself to break away from him. 'Thank you for the last few days. But…I can't… I can't…'

She put her hand up to his face and she touched him, a fleeting gesture, maybe reassuring herself that he was real and not some figment of this magic night, this magic setting.

'I need to ground myself,' she faltered. 'I need to return to my islanders, my medicine and my son. I need…to go.'

'Do you?'

'Yes.'

'Lily—'

'No. No, please. You can't... And neither can I.'

She was right and he knew it. They both knew it. And she at least had the courage of her convictions.

This night was meant for them, he thought, but he could take it no further.

They both knew it. Before he could say another word she fled. She grabbed her sandals and her picnic basket as she ran up the beach, and then she disappeared into the night, behind the palms, back to her bungalow. Back to her life.

As she must.

As he must return to his life. For it was what he wanted. Wasn't it? He stared once more at the magic light show put on just for them.

'Find another audience, guys,' he said wearily. 'You misjudged this one.'

But how could she find sleep after that? She couldn't. The night was long and full of shadows, and Ben was no longer beside her.

She had Benjy back, she told herself. It should be enough. But Ben had lain with her in those nights of terror and she missed the warmth of him, the smell of him. She missed...Ben.

If she'd stayed at the beach...

Don't go there.

The night stretched on and Lily let her thoughts drift to the first time she'd met him. She'd been in her second year of university, studying furiously, her work taking up every available minute. Up three steps of a library ladder, she'd tugged out a tome that had been shoved in too tightly. The book had come out too fast, and all of a sudden she had toppled backward.

But Ben had been right underneath, ready to catch her. She'd landed in his arms; she looked up into his concerned eyes and she'd been smitten. He had been big and dark, with jet-black hair that curled randomly, flopping over his lovely brown eyes and making him look very, very sexy. He had been tall and big-boned and superbly muscled, and he'd had a smile to die for.

'Hey, the sky's falling!' he'd exclaimed, holding her close. 'But who's complaining if the sky looks like this?' He'd set her on her feet and he'd chuckled and brushed curls out of her eyes and picked up her books—and she'd fallen in love on the spot.

The years that followed were amazing. Ben took life as it came, seizing every opportunity with both hands. Oh, he was hard-working—his medicine was as important to him as it was to Lily—but from that day their mutual studies became fun. They studied together, they surfed, they went bushwalking, they drank coffee in late-night bars, they argued long into the night over anything and everything. It was a magical few years that almost blew her away with happiness.

But there was no long-term commitment. Ben's background was wealth and neglect—his parents were socialites who threw money at their son instead of affection. And there was more. Lily guessed at shadows he wouldn't talk of, and he wouldn't let her probe.

And Lily? Lily had been taught what love did and she'd thought she didn't want it. Her mother had abandoned the island and her people for a handsome Frenchman. When he walked out, Lily was four and mother and child were left destitute. Lily still had hazy memories of those days, which had culminated in her mother's attempted suicide when she was seven. French authorities contacted the islanders and Lily and her mother were brought home, to be accepted back with love but to know that the island was not to be lightly left. And to be taught by her mother that romantic love was catastrophic.

So she'd agreed with Ben that love was for others. She'd tried to mean it, too, but she'd failed. Her heart was irrevocably his, but there was no way she could tell him. She might love him, but she agreed there was no future for them. For when med school was complete she knew what she had to do.

And she'd done it, she told herself. She'd come home. And she'd borne Benjy—who looked like his daddy.

Benjy stirred now in his sleep and she kissed the top of his head. The resemblance was amazing.

'When Ben leaves again, I'll still have you,' she whispered, but it wasn't enough.

It had to be enough. For ever.

She had been right to leave the beach tonight, she told herself. She had to be right.

And Ben…

Back in his quarters, listening to Sam's not so gentle snoring, Ben was no closer to sleep than Lily.

What was wrong with him? He usually slept the moment his head hit the pillow.

Not now. He was thinking of Lily. Lily spinning slowly in her pool of phosphorescence. Lily.

Her face was right before him, the strain behind her eyes deep and real. The medical needs on this island were huge. She'd been working too hard before this had happened. And now… He'd leave her and she'd sink back into a life where duty overcame all.

She should have time off. That much was obvious. For her to calmly go on working with no time to adjust was asking for long-term trouble.

They had to get a medical team here on a longer-term basis, he thought. Well, maybe he could arrange that. In this current climate, no reasonable request would be refused. He could get doctors and paramedics here for at least the next few months.

That wouldn't stop Lily working.

But she had to stop working. He thought again of the strain behind her eyes. She'd collapse if she didn't stop.

She needed more nights like tonight, he thought. Oh, not with him, but nights where she could stop spinning because of work.

And then…

An idea came into his mind, so preposterous that for a moment he almost rejected it unexamined. She wouldn't.

But she needed it so much.

He thought of the island's political head. Gualberto Panjiamtu was a man in his seventies, who'd coped with being held hostage with dignity, and had emerged with his concern for his islanders paramount. Gualberto would understand that Lily's health was vital to all. Could he ask Gualberto to release Lily from her obligations for a while?

She'd never agree.

But ideas kept spinning, faster than Lily had spun on the beach.

He should sleep.

He didn't sleep. He lay and stared at the canvas overhead, and thought. About Lily.

CHAPTER SIX

LILY didn't see Ben all the next day. So much for Ben getting to know Benjy. Benjy stayed with her as she moved through the island, spending time with each of the traumatised islanders, trying to prevent long-term damage.

Normally whenever she visited island homes Benjy would dart off as soon as she arrived, blending with the familiarity of an extended family. But not now. He clung, listening in as the islanders talked through their terrors. He shouldn't be with her, Lily thought. He needed urgent attention himself, but what could she do? With Kira gone, Benjy clung to her as a lifeline and pushing him away would do more harm than allowing him to stay.

She should stay at home with him. But who else would do this? These were her people. She felt like she was being torn in two.

There was nothing to do except to work on through it, so she kept on doing what came next, and by her side Benjy was stoic.

She needed to get her life in order, she thought dully as she and Benjy walked home at dusk. But how? There were no answers.

As they approached her bungalow she saw her lights were on. Often the islanders would come to her house if they needed her. Surely not more work, she thought bleakly.

She was so tired.

'You can do this, Lily,' she murmured, and pushed her door wide.

There was indeed someone waiting for her.

It was Gualberto.

And Ben.

'Gualberto,' she said, setting Ben's presence aside as too confusing. Gualberto, as head of Kapua's council, was a stable presence, a surety in a world that was no longer sure. 'It's lovely that you're here,' she told him, and she meant it. 'How can I help you?'

'It's not for you to help me, Lily,' the old man said gravely. 'It's how I can help you. Ben tells me you need to rest.'

She flashed Ben a look of anger. He hadn't been near Benjy. So much for promises, and now to tell Gualberto she needed to rest... He was piling more problems on an elderly man who had enough to cope with. 'I don't,' she snapped.

'Hear us out, Lily,' Ben said, and she bit her lip.

'Go run a bath, Benjy,' she told her son, but Gualberto put out his hands and tugged her son onto the seat beside him.

'Benjy needs to hear what we've organised.'

'I hope you've organised nothing.'

'We've organised you a holiday, Lily,' the old man said, and he suddenly sounded severe. 'Sit down.'

This was so unusual a statement that she did sit. Benjy was on the chair by Gualberto. It was a four-chair table. That meant she had to sit by Ben.

She sat but she shifted her chair as far away from him as possible.

Gualberto smiled at the movement, as if he found it amusing. What was funny about it? Lily asked herself, and then decided she was too tired to care. She wanted them all to go away. She could sleep for a hundred years.

'There's a thing called burn-out,' Gualberto told her, and

his hand came across the table to grip hers. 'Ben tells me you have it.'

'Ben doesn't know me.' She tried to tug her hand away but she couldn't.

'Ben has organised for you to take a rest,' the old man said sternly. 'We've thought this thing through. We depend on you, and we've pushed this dependence too far.'

'I don't know what you mean.' This feeling of being out of control…she'd had it since that first morning when the finance councillor had stumbled, wounded, through her front door, and it was growing stronger rather than weakening. She felt as if her body was growing so light that any minute she could float free.

She felt terrified.

Maybe something of what she was feeling showed in her face, for the old man's sternness lessened. 'Lily, you're not to try any longer,' he said gently. 'After medical school you came home to work here, on this island, but as the outer islands have discovered we have a permanent doctor, they've been using you, too. Your workload has built to the stage where you can no longer cope. It's taken Dr Blayden to show us that.'

'He doesn't know—'

'I do, Lily.' Ben looked concerned, as he had no right to be on her behalf. 'Sam and I have been looking through the records of hospital admissions.'

'You had no right—'

'And we've talked to the island nurses. You're doing ten clinics a week, seven of them on outer islands. You're on call twenty-four hours a day, seven days a week. The hospital is nearly always full because the islanders refuse to go else-where—why should they when they have you to care for them? You're doing the work of three doctors.'

'Meanwhile, Kira's been caring for Benjy,' Gualberto said. 'And now Kira's dead.'

'Mama looks after me,' Benjy interjected, trying to keep up with what was happening, and Gualberto nodded in agreement.

'Of course she does. That's what mothers do. But your mama takes care of all the islanders as well.'

'She still has to look after me,' Benjy said.

Lily heard panic and rose and rounded the table and tugged him into her arms.

'Of course I do. Of course I will.'

'Some things go without saying,' Gualberto said heavily. 'But, Benjy, your mother's had a dreadful time, and we need to take care of her as she takes care of us.'

'I—I don't know what y-you mean,' Lily stammered, but Gualberto was pushing himself heavily to his feet. He'd had a dreadful time, too, these past days, and it showed.

'Lily, I can't heal anything,' he said. 'But I'll do my best. I know who Ben is and what he is to you.' He looked at Benjy and back at Ben, as if confirming the undeniable resemblance. 'There are many things you need to sort out, but one thing is already sorted. Ben is a good man. He *is* a good man, Lily,' he reiterated heavily. 'I know the men he works with and I know him myself. I've watched him work with our people in the time since he arrived and I tell this to you strongly—he is a good man, as Jacques never was. Maybe that's none of my business but I have accepted his proposal on your behalf.'

'Proposal?' She flashed a glance of pure astonishment at Ben.

'We haven't paid you as we ought,' the old man said heavily. 'When you returned after medical school we had a subsistence economy. You agreed to work for a tiny wage plus a share of the necessities we all share in. That seemed reasonable. But now… Ben asked me if you could afford to go away for a little and I had to tell him you couldn't.' He grimaced. 'Maybe we've been too afraid of what the oil money would do to us. Maybe we were too fearful of Jacques and his intentions. Regardless, what money we have is tied up in the short term.'

'That's nothing to do with—'

'It is something to do with you,' he went on, inexorable now he'd started. 'For there's no money to say to you go where you want. But there is an alternative.'

'I don't want an alternative.'

'Listen, Lily,' Ben said urgently and Lily subsided again. A little.

'Ben tells us that he owns a farm on the coast of New South Wales,' Gualberto said. 'This is what he proposes, and I agree. There's nothing there but a housekeeper and farm manager. Ben tells me there's a beach, horses to ride and nothing to do. Nothing, Lily. You will stay there for a month.'

'I can't.' She was staring wildly from Gualberto to Ben and back again. Were they out of their minds? To propose that she just leave…

And go to Ben's property?

'Ben will stay here to cope with medical necessities,' Gualberto said, interjecting before the next obvious objection was aired. 'Maybe he'll join you toward the end of your stay, but not before. He says you and Benjy need space to be by yourselves. We all agree.'

She opened her mouth but Ben was there before her.

'Think it through, Lily,' he said urgently, his eyes never leaving hers. 'I'll organise the medical set-up here. I'm due for leave and I'll take it as such, so even if there's a crisis I can't be called away. Officially Sam will stay on for a bit as well, and three of our nurses want to stay. With your people that's a full medical complement.'

'But…you can't just do that,' she faltered. 'You can't just walk in and say go to some farm I've never heard of.'

'Would you not like to get away, Lily?' Gualberto asked her, serious now, pushing for an answer. 'Truly, Lily? In your heart?'

'I don't… I don't…'

'You do,' Ben said. 'You're desperate for a break and you know it. Benjy needs time with you. Just say yes, my love.'

'I'm not your love,' she whispered, dazed.

'Of course not,' he said ruefully. 'I meant…Lily. Just say yes, Dr Cyprano.'

'A farm?' Benjy whispered. He'd been trying desperately to keep up and he thought he had it now. 'We can go to a farm, Mama.'

'Just say yes,' Ben repeated, and Gualberto smiled at them all and made to leave.

'I think the yes is already spoken,' he said gravely. 'Lily, for the next few weeks you're forbidden to practise medicine anywhere on this group of islands. We love you as our own but for the next few weeks you belong to yourself. Take your son and go. And now…' He smiled, a world-weary smile that still managed to hold a hint of real amusement. 'I'll move on to the next problem, but I believe I don't need to worry more about this one. I'll leave you in the capable hands of Dr Blayden.'

Ben stayed on. She asked him to leave but he simply shook his head and started making dinner.

'I can do this,' she told him, but he shook his head. She was sitting, stunned, at her kitchen table while this big man in army camouflage took over her life.

'I've found three casseroles in the refrigerator,' he told her. 'The one that looks best says it's red emperor in spicy coconut cream broth.' He grinned at Benjy, man to man. 'Red emperor'd be fish? I reckon that'd be guaranteed to put hairs on your chest. How about it?'

Benjy looked at Ben and then cautiously at his mother. Then he tugged the neck of his T-shirt forward and looked down at his hairless tummy.

He glanced again at Ben—who grinned some more and flipped a couple of buttons open, baring his chest to the waist. Definitely hairy.

'Like me,' he said. 'There's a heap of fish and coconut cream gone into this manly chest.'

'You're mad,' Lily said faintly, trying to block out the vision of a body any young boy would think was enviable. Though who was she kidding? It wasn't Benjy who thought it was fantastic. She so wanted to...

No. She wouldn't listen to her hormones, she told herself fiercely, while Benjy agreed that maybe he did want some of the casserole.

They ate together. Mostly they ate in silence, though occasionally Ben would direct a remark to Benjy, which Benjy would consider and answer with a monosyllabic reply. Ben didn't appear put out by the lack of conversation. He attacked the truly excellent casserole with relish, then cleared away while Lily sat, still stunned, seemingly unable to move.

Ben's farm, her mind was saying. No.

But... Get away, her heart was replying, and it sounded so desirable it was like a siren's song. Where were earmuffs when she needed them? And as well as that...

Ben's farm. That suddenly wasn't her mind talking. It was her heart.

Ben could be there at the end of their stay, just for a little. Benjy might get to know his father. At the end of the time she'd come back here and get on with the rest of her life, but Benjy might have established a relationship. Which he needed to have.

This was crazy. She couldn't leave. These were her people.

Benjy slumped in weariness almost before he finished his dinner. Trying her best to ignore Ben—she didn't know what else to do—she carried him through to bed. He was asleep before his head hit the pillow. She gazed down at his small face for a long moment and then turned to find Ben watching.

'You must let him have a break,' Ben said gently. 'You can't move forward from this as if nothing has happened.'

'You're a psychologist?'

'I've talked to psychologists.'

'What gives you the right—?'

'He's my son.'

She drew in her breath, but it was as if she didn't find any. Once more that disembodied feeling came over her, as if she was floating, out of control.

Maybe she swayed, she didn't know, but all of a sudden he was right before her, lifting her into his arms, holding her against him for a brief, hard moment, letting her feel the strength of his body against her—grounding her—and then lowering her gently onto the bed beside Benjy.

She didn't know how. She didn't know why. But it worked. The awful dizziness faded and she felt the pillow soft and cool against her face. For one crazy moment she considered giving in to this man—doing what he said—letting him take a control she no longer had.

It was a crazy thought, but right now she didn't have the capacity to fight it.

'Do you know how close to collapse you are?' Ben growled, and she thought about that, or tried to think, but things were a bit fuzzy. He was so…male, she thought inconsequentially. Nice.

Tomorrow she'd be sensible and tell him what he could do with his preposterous idea, she decided. Tonight… Tonight he was glaring down at her, concerned, and she thought how wonderful it was to have someone concerned about her. It was her whose job it was to be concerned about everyone on this island, and on every other island within boating distance. Now the tables were turned.

'I'm not close to collapse,' she managed, and Ben's gorgeous brown eyes crinkled into laughter, the laughter she'd always loved.

'Of course you're not,' he agreed. 'You could run a ten-mile race right now.'

'Maybe ten yards?' she said cautiously, and he chuckled.

'Maybe not even one foot from your pillow. You're going on this holiday, my lovely Lily. I've set it up for you. The islanders have agreed. There are people to take over your work… Lily, have you ever had time off with Benjy?'

How could she think about that when his eyes were on hers and the pillow was soft and Benjy was warm against her and Ben was…Ben was there?

'I don't—'

'That's what I've been told,' he said, and his smile faded. 'Don't fight me on this one, Lily. Tomorrow we're putting you on a helicopter out of here. We're taking two of our injured back to Sydney Central and then the pilot will take you to the farm. It's *en route* to base so there's no problem. Rosa and Doug, my farm managers, are expecting you. You're to spend the next few weeks healing our son and healing yourself.'

Our son.

Lily gazed at Ben for a long moment. *Our son*.

She should resent the words, she thought, but instead… It seemed as if she was handing over control. That was something she'd vowed never to do, but now it was happening it wasn't the void she'd feared. The lightness was with her again but instead of making her feel ill it suddenly felt like there might just be a sliver of joy in all this.

'No argument,' Ben told her.

How could she argue? She couldn't even raise her head from the pillow.

'You're so done in,' Ben said ruefully, and he knelt by the bed and touched her cheek with his forefinger. It was like a caress, a gesture of warmth and strength and caring. The feeling was an illusion, she thought, but for now she didn't care. She'd take her comfort where she could find it.

'No argument for tonight,' she whispered.

'That's great.' He sounded relieved.

She thought dreamily, Why was he relieved? As if she could ever argue with him.

But, of course, she could. She must. But not tonight.

'I'll argue tomorrow,' she whispered, and he smiled.

'It won't help. But you're welcome to try. Goodnight, my Lily,' he said, and he bent suddenly and kissed her, hard on the mouth, as she remembered being kissed all those years ago. She should push him away. She should…

But she didn't. The kiss lasted for as long as she wanted, a delicious, languorous indulgence in sensual pleasure that surely should have had her running back to her tightly controlled world. Men were dangerous. Ben was dangerous.

But not tonight. Tonight she let him kiss her. She even found the energy to put her arms around his neck, to hold his head in her hands, to deepen the kiss and to take what she needed.

Delicious, languorous pleasure.

She was almost asleep. It had to end, but when it did, when he finally pulled away, her eyes were closing on a lovely dream. Her world was right. Ben was there.

Which was a ridiculous thing to think, but think it she did and it pervaded her dreams. She snuggled against Benjy and she slept as she hadn't slept for a long, long time.

And kneeling beside her, Ben kept watch over Lily and her son—*his* son—until his pager crackled into life, until there were medical imperatives and he could watch no more.

CHAPTER SEVEN

SHE woke up and he was gone. For a moment the remnants of her dream stayed with her, making her smile, making her look expectantly to where Ben had been. But, of course, he wasn't there.

She glanced at her bedside clock—and found it wasn't there either. Startled, she checked her wristwatch—and yelped.

It was eight-thirty. There was a ward round to be done and…

And things were different. Benjy was awake. She focused on the rest of her bedroom. Benjy had pulled an ancient suitcase from the bottom of the wardrobe. He had a pile of clothes folded beside him and he was calmly assessing each item.

'Hi,' she said cautiously, and he turned and smiled at her. It was a great smile. It was a smile she hadn't seen for too long.

'Ben came round a while ago,' Benjy said. 'When he thought we were asleep he was going to go away again, but I heard him and we had toast together. He said I should start thinking about what I'll need to take to the farm.'

The farm idea hadn't been a dream, then. But it might as well be. The idea was crazy.

'We'll talk about it after I'm dressed,' she told him. 'Benjy, we need to—'

'Ben says Sam's doing house calls this morning,' Benjy told her. 'And the nice nurse with the funny-coloured hair. Yellow and green. Debbie. Ben said Sam and Debbie are going to sort out all our problems, no sweat.'

'Did he say that?' she said, starting for the bathroom. 'As if he knows.'

'He says we're leaving at ten and if we're not ready he's going to pick us up and toss us in the helicopter and take us regardless.' He stared down at two T-shirts. 'I don't know what regardless means. Mama, which one should I pack?'

'Neither.'

'Don't you want us to go?'

'Benjy, we can't.'

'There will be horses,' Benjy whispered. 'Ben said there will be horses and I can ride one.'

Drat the man. How dared he upset her son?

'Horses smell. And they kick. Did Ben take away my alarm clock?'

'Ben's horses wouldn't kick and I don't like your alarm clock.'

'Neither do I, sweetheart,' she told him. 'But it's all about who I am.'

'I want a holiday,' he said, suddenly stubborn. 'The children in my picture books have holidays. I want one.'

Lily's resolve faltered. She hesitated and there was a sharp rap on the outside door. It opened before she could respond, and Ben was there, dressed in his camouflage gear again, looking big and tough and dangerous. And smiling.

'Why are you wearing those clothes?' she said, trying to sound cross and not breathless. 'You look like you're heading into battle.'

'Believe it or not, I don't have anything else,' he told her. 'I didn't pop in an extra bag of casual gear.'

'I like it,' Benjy announced. 'I want to wear a uniform like that when I grow up.'

'No, you don't,' Lily told him, but her son looked suddenly mutinous. Uh-oh.

'What are you doing here?' she demanded, thinking maybe this was a dangerous conversation to pursue—though concentrating on Ben rather than Benjy seemed even riskier.

'I came to wake you up,' he said cheerfully. 'I didn't want you to sleep through your holiday.'

'You took my alarm clock.'

'Guilty, but it was an entirely altruistic action on my part, as here I am, replacing it. Wouldn't you rather wake up to me?'

'No,' she snapped, but his grin was making her think he had a point. He definitely had a point. 'Anyway, you make a lousy substitute. My clock was set for six.'

'A perfectly ridiculous time,' he told her. 'For the first day of your holiday.'

'Ben, I'm not—'

'Lily, you are,' he told her, and his smile faded. 'I meant what I said last night. If you could afford some other way of doing this—of getting away from the island a bit by yourself—and I thought you would, then maybe I wouldn't be this bossy. But all the islanders agree.'

'All…'

'Every single person I've talked to,' he said cheerfully. 'Bar none. The women want to pack for you but I figured you only needed spare knickers and togs.'

'Togs?'

'Swimsuit,' he said patiently. 'Honestly, Lily, you spent six years in Australia.'

'I know what togs are. Ben, I can't.'

He'd come to the bedroom door but no further, which was just as well. She'd woken some time in the night and had tugged off her pants and bra. She was now wearing a pair of very scanty knickers and a T-shirt that didn't come down quite far enough.

This man was the father of her child, she told herself, feeling desperate. He knew her so well that appearing before him in knickers and T-shirt shouldn't worry her.

It did. She wanted all the barricades she could get, and clothing was just the start of it.

'Lily, you can.' Still he didn't move. He's holding himself back, she thought. He's feeling the same as I am.

'Just in case you do want to take more than knickers and togs, Pieter's wife's here to help you pack,' he told her. He turned back and Mary was behind him. She came in now, cautiously, as if she was afraid what she might find, but when she saw Lily in her knickers and T-shirt she smiled, her broad islander face a tonic all on its own.

'You dress well to greet your visitors,' she said, and Lily glared at both of them.

'Mary, tell Ben he has no right ordering me around.'

'He does have a right,' Mary said softly. 'I'm here as back-up. I'm here to tell you we all agree. You were exhausted before this happened. All of us knew it. We just chose to ignore it because…well, maybe we needed you too much. But we don't need you now. You're to go, child. Take your Benjy and do what the good doctor says. You're not to come back before you've gained ten pounds and you've lost those dark shadows under yours eyes.'

'Mary—'

'Don't argue,' she said severely, and then rounded on Ben. 'What are you doing here?' she demanded. 'Lily needs to shower and pack and there's no room in that for you. Shoo.'

'Yes, ma'am,' Ben said, and he grinned and blew a kiss to Lily—and shooed.

An hour and a half later, Lily and her son were in the great army helicopter, heading for the mainland. She had to work during the journey. That was how Ben had squared it with the authorities—indeed, it suited them all well. A corporal with shrapnel in her knee and a supply sergeant who'd smashed a hip in the chaos of the night of the helicopters both needed constant medical attention, but they wanted to go home to Sydney.

So Benjy sat up front with the pilot, one half of him overjoyed to be right where he was and the other half of him thinking holiday, holiday, holiday, horses, horses, horses. Lily worked on in the rear. One part of her was still a doctor, checking her patients were comfortable, making sure there was no deterioration, talking to them about their condition and how they were looking forward to being reunited with their families. One tiny part of Lily was thinking holiday. But the biggest part was thinking Ben, Ben, Ben, and there was no way she could get the refrain from her head.

Ben watched the chopper disappear from view and it was as if he'd cut out a part from himself and sent it with them.

Lily and his son.

'You should be with them, mate.' It was Sam, coming up behind him and placing a hand on his shoulder. The sensation made Ben start and Sam grinned.

'You're not very awake, are you, lad? I could be the enemy.'

'There's no enemy here. Not any more.'

'No.' Sam eyed the retreating helicopter thoughtfully. 'So tell me again—why didn't you go with them?'

'I need to work here.'

'I'm working here.'

'So that makes two of us. Plus the nurses. It's what we need.'

'So let's see if I'm right,' Sam said thoughtfully. 'You've sent the lady to your family farm. You've also volunteered to take leave because you know the powers that be won't approve two doctors staying here, and the lady wouldn't have gone if she didn't know there were two of us to take over her work.'

'That's—'

'The truth,' Sam said. 'You've got it bad, mate.'

'I haven't got anything.'

'You're still in love with her.'

'She's gorgeous,' Ben snapped. 'Anyone would love her.'

'She used to be gorgeous,' Sam said bluntly. 'Now she's skinny. She's got too many freckles, her hair needs a decent cut and she looks like she hasn't slept for a month.'

'That's why she needs a holiday.'

'Yeah, but it doesn't say she's gorgeous.' He hesitated. 'You planning on following this through?'

'Like how?'

'The kid's yours,' Sam said. 'You marry her and you have an instant family. How does that seem?'

'It won't happen.'

'Why not?'

'I don't do family.'

'No,' Sam said thoughtfully. 'Of course you don't.'

'Look, can we leave this?' Ben said, exasperated. 'You're planning on operating on Larry Arnoo this afternoon?'

'Yeah,' Sam said, and grimaced. 'Larry should be on his way to Sydney, too. There's shrapnel too close to the spine to leave it there. If it hits a nerve he's stuffed. But there's no way he's going to Sydney. He's only agreed to have the operation here because he assumed Lily would do it.'

'As if she could.'

'Have you seen some of the work she's done on this island?' Sam demanded. 'She and Pieter—a nurse with no formal training whatsoever—have done operations in the past that would have made me quake. Because there's no one else to do them.'

'She's out of it now,' Ben growled. 'She has a month off, or more if I can manage it.'

'But you're not interested in marrying her?'

'Hell, Sam, I don't do marriage. And do you think she'd follow me where I go for the rest of her life? Or stay happily a home body while I'm away?'

'No chance.'

'Well, then,' Ben said heavily. 'That's it. We're back where we started. Long-term friends. But at least I won't leave her pregnant this time.'

'Not if you stay here and she stays there,' Sam agreed, and grinned. 'But that's not likely to be a long-term arrangement, now, is it?'

CHAPTER EIGHT

THE chopper crew set their patients down at Sydney Central. Benjy watched open-mouthed as Sydney appeared and disappeared underneath them. He didn't say another word until they reached Ben's property.

Neither did Lily. It had been seven years since she'd seen anything but the island, and there was a lot to see. They followed the coast north, until they came to a mountainous region where farms seemed few and far between.

'Here we are,' the pilot called cheerfully, and set the big machine down to land.

A woman seemed to be waiting. They saw her first, a dot beside a house set on coastal farmland. The dot grew bigger until it became the woman.

It must be one of Ben's managers.

In the tiny part of her mind that had dared to think ahead to what waited for them, Lily had imagined some sort of elderly family retainer, a plump and cuddly lady who made sponge cakes and beamed.

No such thing. Sure, Rosa was an older woman—in her sixties maybe?—but there the resemblance to her image stopped. She was thin and wiry, dressed in tight-fitting jeans, glossy boots and a crimson shirt with sleeves rolled up to the elbows. A defiant redhead, with auburn curls twisted into an elegant knot, she looked like some sort of retired Spanish dancer, Lily thought, tugging Benjy out from under the blades while the pilot tossed out their bags. She turned to say goodbye, but the chopper was already rising.

Her escape route was cut.

Benjy was right behind her, clinging as if the woman might bite. Lily took her son's small hand and propelled him forward, and then thought she was almost using her small son as a shield. She had that light-headed feeling of being out of control again.

Oh, for heaven's sake… This was nothing to worry about.

'Hi,' the woman called without a trace of a Spanish accent, and there was the second illusion dispelled. 'Welcome to Nurrumbeen.'

Nurrumbeen. All she knew of this place was what she'd seen as they'd circled before landing. It was a farm seemingly carved into the wilderness, rich grazing land encircled by sea on one side and rainforest on the other.

What on earth was she going to do here for a month? No people. No medicine. She wouldn't have minded the odd shop, she soundlessly told the absent Ben, and the thought of his possible reaction to such a whinge was enough to allow her to greet Rosa with a smile.

'We're Lily and Benjy. I hope you're expecting us.'

'We surely are.' Rosa shook Lily's hand with a grip as strong as a man's and then her eyes moved past her to Benjy. 'Benjy,' she whispered in a tone that said she either knew or she guessed Ben's involvement. There was intelligence in these black eyes. Not much would get past Rosa. 'You're both more welcome than I can say,' she said. 'Come into the house.'

The house was long and low, white-painted, with wide verandas all around and the all-pervasive scent of something that looked like honeysuckle running riot everywhere. They walked inside and there were so many questions in Lily's head that she felt as if she might burst. By her side, Benjy seemed awed into silence.

Ben should be here.

In all the time she'd spent with Ben during university, never once had he introduced her to his parents or taken her to any of the properties his parents owned. Neither had he talked about his family. 'We don't get on,' he'd said brusquely, and she'd never got past it. For her to come here now, with his son…

Without him…

There was a man inside, older than Rosa, small, wiry and greying. He was leaning heavily on a walking stick—and he was wearing an apron.

'This is my Doug,' Rosa said proudly, as if conjuring up something magical. 'We're here to look after you.'

'You're…Ben's parents' housekeepers?' Lily asked cautiously, and Lily and Doug both smiled.

'I'm Ben's housekeeper,' Doug said. 'But food first, questions later.' He sat them down in the big farmhouse kitchen and produced sandwiches, sponge cake and chocolate éclairs. Rosa poured tea for Lily and lemonade for Benjy and both Rosa and Doug beamed as they ate and drank, seeming to enjoy the fact that they were obviously disconcerted.

Ben *should* be here, Lily thought again. This is his house. Or…is this his parents' house?

'I'm not sure what the set-up is here,' she ventured, as Benjy wrapped himself around a chocolate éclair.

'Tell it like it is, Rosa.' Doug pushed another éclair forward and Lily couldn't resist. Yum.

'We're housekeeper and farm manager,' Rosa told her. 'Doug's the housekeeper—he makes the best sponge cakes you've ever eaten.' She hesitated then, glancing at Doug and then nodding, as if coming to a decision to tell more.

'Doug was a farmhand here when he was young and I worked in the stables,' Rosa told them. 'Ben's parents were running the place as a horse stud but they spent very little time here. But we knew Ben when he was little. And his sister.'

A sister. Lily's eyes widened. She'd dated Ben for years. What else didn't she know? 'I didn't know Ben had a sister.'

'Bethany died when she was four,' Rosa said. 'But by then Ben was at boarding school. Anyway, when Ben was about twelve Doug had an appalling tractor accident.'

'It rolled on top of me,' Doug said, smiling at Benjy, as if trying to make light of what must have been dreadful. 'Damned wheel mount gave way on a slope. You ever thought how much a two-ton tractor can hurt? One day I'll show you the scars.'

'Wow,' whispered Benjy through cream.

'Anyway, Ben's parents wouldn't accept liability,' Rosa said, without rancour, stating facts. 'They said it was Doug's duty to maintain the tractor—the fact that there'd been no money to maintain it was carefully ignored and they doctored their bank accounts to make it seem like there was. There was a court case and we lost. The fight left us in debt for years. We left here. I worked in a racing stable and Doug...well, Doug stayed home and tried to keep himself occupied.'

'I learned how to cook,' Doug said.

'He did,' Rosa said affectionately. 'Then about six years ago Ben's father passed away. His mother had died earlier and it wasn't a month after his father's death before Ben came to find us.'

'He remembered us,' Doug said, smiling at a memory he obviously found good. 'His parents didn't come here often but until my accident they'd send Ben. He'd arrive on his own for holidays.'

'Like us,' Benjy announced, and Doug nodded.

'Exactly like you. Rosa taught him to ride a horse.'

'And he remembered us all those years later,' Rosa said softly. 'Until his parents died there was little he could do, but as soon as he could, he did.'

'What did he do?' Lily asked.

'He installed us back here,' Rosa said with quiet pride. 'There's a little house behind this one—it's beautiful. He's given us life tenancy. He sat and talked about what Doug and I could do and we said I loved the farm and Doug could keep a house clean. So that's what we are. Housekeeper and farm manager.'

'You should see me hoover,' Doug said, grinning, and Lily suddenly felt like grinning back. For the last week she'd been moving in a nightmare. This couple made her feel she was waking up. And Ben's care…

She'd fallen in love with him all those years ago. Suddenly she was remembering why.

'Does Ben come here often now?' she asked, and Rosa gave a definite nod.

'Whenever he can. We keep telling him he should bring friends here—girlfriends and the like—but he won't.'

'He's a bit of a loner, and he's not the marrying kind,' Doug added, but Rosa's eyes had moved to Benjy.

'Maybe he hasn't been until now,' she said. 'But things change.' Her gaze shifted to Lily. 'Do you and he—?'

'Leave the girl alone, love,' Doug said, starting to clear the table. 'No questions. You know what Ben said. She's worn to the bone. Just food and rest and plenty of both. Starting now. Rosa, take them to their bedrooms for a nap before they explore the farm.'

'Yes, sir.' Rosa clicked her riding boots together as she saluted her husband. Then she smiled and waited for Lily and Benjy to accompany her. 'Let's get you settled for a really long stay.'

* * *

They were at his farm.

Ben had several properties, left to him by parents who had valued everything in terms of money. Nurrumbeen was the only place he had any emotional tie to, and it was only his sense of obligation to Doug and Rosa that had created that tie.

He'd go there when he had the medicine on the island thoroughly sorted, he told himself.

But wanted to go there now.

Why?

Benjy was his kid, he thought as the days wore on. He had to learn to kick a football. He had to learn to ride a horse.

Rosa would teach him to ride.

Maybe it'd be fun to teach him himself.

But that meant involvement. The kid might even learn to need him.

He didn't do needing. He couldn't. It'd do his head in. He was a man who walked alone.

Until now, a little voice whispered insidiously in his head. You could stop and be a family.

And keep on doing the work I love?

You could change direction. You might even learn to love other things.

Which was a really scary thought. He thought back to his childhood. Every single thing he'd ever loved had been a fleeting attachment—to people like Rosa and Doug, people he had seen when his parents had allowed it and then who'd disappeared out of his life forever. Like his sister. Bethany. That's what love is, he thought bleakly. He knew enough now to shield himself from it.

If he loved, he lost.

Forget it. You have work to do here, he told himself severely. Stay here, stick to your medicine and get them out of your mind.

As if.

* * *

For the first three days Lily threw herself into her holiday as if she only had days to get to experience everything. She rode, she fished, she swam, she built the world's biggest sandcastle, she read late into the night, she rose at dawn to jog on the beach…

Rosa and Doug watched and said little. Benjy was drawn to them, she knew. They offered to take over his care and let her rest, but rest wasn't on her agenda. Neither was clinging to her son, but her legacy from the last few days was one of fear, and everywhere she went, Benjy went, too.

Benjy loved the horses. Rosa and Doug grazed beef cattle— that was the farm's main income—but Rosa had four mares and one stallion—just to give her pleasure—and they gave Benjy pleasure, too.

One of the mares was heavily pregnant and Benjy was fascinated. 'We can't go until Flicker's had her foal,' he told Lily, and Lily thought she wasn't sure how long she could stand being there.

She was still in overdrive, playing as hard as she'd worked on the island. The events of the past few days haunted her. The effects they'd had on Benjy haunted her as well, making her worried sick that there might be long-term repercussions. He hardly talked to her of the time in the compound. He hardly spoke of Kira. He never spoke of Jacques.

She'd betrayed her son by loving Jacques. Or…by thinking she'd loved Jacques?

She hardly slept.

'You're like a wound-up clockwork toy,' Rosa said on the third night. Doug was feeding the dogs, Benjy was supervising and Lily and Rosa were picking peas from the vegetable patch. 'Why don't you go for a walk by yourself after dinner? Let Doug read to the boy. It'd do them both good.' Her smile faded a little. 'I worry about Doug.'

'Why?'

'He has chest pain.'

Lily frowned. 'What sort of chest pain? Do you want me to talk to him? You know I'm a doctor.'

'No.' Rosa grimaced. 'He'd hate it that I said anything. He hardly admits it to me, and I'm sure it's worse than he lets me see.' She hesitated. 'But when Ben comes…maybe Ben will do something.'

'Rosa, if it really is chest pain, he needs urgent medical assessment.'

'If he goes to the doctor when Ben's not here and the doctor says he has to stop doing housework then we'll leave here,' Rosa said, sounding desperate. 'After Ben's been so good to us there's no way Doug would stay on if he can't work for his keep.' She hesitated. 'But maybe if it was Ben that was to do the telling… I know it sounds foolish but pride's one of the few things left to Doug.'

'Rosa, chest pain can mean—'

'There's nothing you can do or I can do,' Rosa said with finality. 'We wait for Ben. And as for now, you're to go for a walk. Ben says you should.'

'When did he tell you that?' she demanded, startled, and Rosa smiled.

'He rang us when you were at the beach. He worries about you.'

Then, as if on cue, the phone rang again. 'What's the bet this'll be Ben?' Doug called from the veranda. 'Rosa told him this morning that you wouldn't slow down, and he's worried.'

Suddenly she found she was shaking. Maybe Ben was right, she conceded. Maybe she was cracking up.

'It *is* Ben,' Doug called.

She walked up the steps to the kitchen. Rosa and Benjy followed. So much for privacy. They were all watching her. She turned her back on the lot of them. Rosa, Doug and Benjy were gazing at her as if she was their evening's entertainment.

She *was* cracking up.

'Hi,' she said, and took a deep breath and tried again. 'Hi.' That was better. Her voice didn't squeak this time.

'Rosa says you're running on overdrive,' Ben said.

Lily thought, Great, cut to the chase, why don't you?

'I'm fine,' she told him. 'I need to come home.'

'The island's OK without you,' he said softly, as if he understood where her head was, which was crazy for how could he know? 'Sam and Pieter and I have the medicine here under control. You're not coming home until you're well.'

'I am well.'

'You're not well. I want you to do something for me.'

'Not unless I can come home.'

He chuckled, that deep throaty chuckle that had once made her smile but now suddenly made her want to weep. 'It's not going to happen, sweetheart,' he said.

'Don't call me—'

'Lily,' he corrected himself. 'If I've figured out the time difference right, you should be just about to have dinner.'

'How did—?'

'Doug's meals are like clockwork.'

'How often do you come here?'

'We're talking about you. Not me.'

'We shouldn't be.'

'Just shut up for a minute. If you go out straight after dinner—'

'I can't.'

'Let me speak,' he said, exasperated. 'There's a track from the house to the ridge up on Blair Peak. It's a full moon here so it's a full moon there as well. We're under the same moon, Lily. Remember that. Anyway, I want you to put some decent boots on and take yourself up to the peak.'

'Tonight?'

'Tonight,' he said. 'Sit up at the peak for as long as you need. Then walk straight down to the beach and wander back with your toes in the water.' She heard his smile again. 'Take your boots off first.'

'Is this some sort of order?'

'It's a medical prescription.'

'Benjy can't—'

'This is not for Benjy,' he said. 'It's for you.'

'It's dumb.'

'It's a medical prescription, Lily,' he repeated, his voice softening. 'Trust me.'

'Why should I?'

'For no reason other than I'm asking,' he said. 'Lily, do this. For you.'

'I can't.'

'Yes, you can, my love. Or, at least, you can try.'

'Don't tell me what to do.'

'OK. I'm not telling. I'm suggesting. You can be angry while you do it, but I still think you should do it.'

And the phone went dead.

She replaced the receiver on its cradle, and turned slowly to face the rest of them. They were all looking at her, expectant, waiting for news. *You can, my love...* He had no right to call her that.

But he had.

'He said I should go up to Blair Peak,' Lily said, noticing in some abstract way that her hand was no longer shaking.

'That's a fine idea,' Rosa approved. 'Wear boots.'

'That's what Ben said.'

'The snakes don't move so much at night,' Doug added. 'But you should err on the side of caution.'

'Snakes,' she whispered, and suddenly her mind was sharp again. 'Are you out of your minds?'

'Nope,' Rosa said cheerfully, dumping peas on the table and starting to pod. 'It's a tiny risk and with boots it's negligible. And so worth it. Ben's right, dear. You have to go.'

'I don't have to do anything.'

'If you want to get well, you need to go,' Doug told her. 'It's better than all the medicine in the world.'

'Go, Mama,' Benjy said. 'You want to be better.'

She stared down at her small son, confounded. 'I'm not sick.'

'No, but you want to be better,' Benjy said. 'It might stop your hands from shaking.'

'So it might,' she whispered. Just how much had her small son noticed?

'There you are, then,' Rosa said, and beamed. 'Benjy, do you want your mama to read you a bedtime story first, or do you want her to go straight after dinner?'

So she went. She hadn't the least idea why she was going, but there were four bulldozers forcing her to go, Rosa and Doug and Benjy—and Ben.

What right did Ben have to propel her to do anything? she demanded of herself, trying to be angry. Trying to be anything but deeply in love with him. But how could she be angry? He'd never been anything but honest with her. And now he'd been the means of sending her to this place, and already Benjy was looking better, the terrors of the past few days becoming something they could face down together.

Regardless, the desire to be angry was still there. The track was easy to follow in the moonlight, but it was steep. She was puffing with effort and kicking stones in front of her as she climbed. Anger was a much simpler emotion to concentrate on than anything else. Anything else was just too darned complicated.

'Just pity the snake that gets in my way,' she said out loud, and then she thought, Lucky it's not Ben who's here, the toad. Pushing her around...

It wasn't working. She tried a bit harder to justify it—and couldn't—and suddenly it was Jacques who was before her.

She'd hardly been able to think of him until now, but suddenly it was Jacques she wanted to kick.

Jacques had seemed caring and compassionate and loving. He'd wooed her for years and she'd finally let herself agree to marry him.

'And you were a criminal,' she said into the darkness. 'You rotten, deceiving toe-rag. You bottom-feeding maw worm.'

She tested out her vocabulary a bit more. That led to frustration. She didn't have the words to match her anger.

Nancy Sinatra's song came into mind, an oldy but a goody—'These Boots Are Made For Walking'. She hummed a few bars and then broke out in song, setting up a squawk in the undergrowth as night creatures were startled out of their peaceful activities.

'Sorry, guys,' she told them, but she sang some more, and suddenly she wasn't thinking about Jacques any more. She was thinking about Ben.

'Well, I don't need you either, you macho army medic.'

Anger faded. She did need Ben.

But he didn't need her.

But then she reached the top, a rocky outcrop at the height of the ridge. Here, for about twenty yards in either direction, no trees grew. She could almost see her island from here, she thought, and she found herself scanning the horizon, looking for home.

There was a rustling in the bushes at the edge of her rock ledge. She turned and a pair of tiny wallabies had broken cover, maybe for no other reason than to look at her. They gazed at her for a long moment. Finally they decided she was harmless and started to crop the mosses at the edges of the rock.

The sky was vast and endless. The moonlight shimmered

over the water. Behind her was the mountain range dividing the coast from the hinterland. It looked as if the whole world was spread out before her.

She felt tiny. Insignificant. She turned to the two wallabies, awed and wanting to share. 'Does this spot put you in your place?' she asked them. They gazed at her, not answering but taking in every detail of what was obviously a very interesting specimen.

'Yes, but a specimen of what?' she whispered.

Ben had sent her up there. 'I'm under the same moon,' he'd said. She let his words drift, and they felt OK. Her island was under the same moon she was under right now. Ben was out there somewhere, caring for her island.

The awful feeling of being bereft, without anchor, without purpose slowly melted.

'Trouble is, he's been under the same moon since the first time I met him,' she whispered. 'I can't get him out of my mind.'

Do you need to?

Maybe we can be friends, she thought, and for a moment felt so bleak that she winced.

But the night wasn't going anywhere. It seemed like she couldn't go down the ridge until she'd thought this through, and the wallabies were waiting for answers.

'He's a good man,' she told them, and they looked as if they might agree. 'He sent me up here.'

It was a bit of a one-way conversation. She needed a bit of feedback, she decided, so she turned back to conversation with herself.

You should have sorted this out seven years ago, she told herself. You know you should. You should have told Ben about Benjy. You should have taught Benjy to care for Ben, and you should have given Ben access. Other parents do that. And maybe you could have even grown to be friends.

It would be good to be Ben's friend.

You don't want to be Ben's friend.

Yes, I do, she told the night, fiercely answering her own accusation. Ben walks alone but that doesn't make him any less of a person. He's a wonderful man and he'll make a wonderful father. Just get things in perspective.

Like how?

Like telling yourself to be sensible. Like admitting you find Ben seriously gorgeous—heck, you know that already. You've had his baby. There's no harm in admitting how sexy you think he is. And if he wants to be part of Benjy's life, you'll see him lots.

That was a good thought. It was even a great thought.

And you can stop feeling guilty, too, she told herself. It wasn't that you were looking for a replacement for Ben that made you accept Jacques. If Ben hadn't been in the back of your mind you probably would have married Jacques a long time ago, and where would that have left you?

Her eyes widened at that. 'So Ben saved me from marrying Jacques,' she whispered. 'Good old Ben. Maybe I should tell him.'

She grinned. She thought about it a little longer, and it felt…OK. 'I'm giving myself my own psychotherapy here,' she told the wallabies. 'Courtesy of Ben.'

She rose, stretched and gazed out to sea. Ben was over there. Just over the horizon.

'I love him,' she told the silence. 'Now I just have to learn to like him.'

You can do that.

'Yes, I can,' she told the wallabies, and she grinned at them both and turned to take the track down the ridge. 'I might have to come up here a few times and talk to you guys again but, hey, you're cheap. Now, if you don't mind, I have a holiday to start.'

How the hell had she done all this?

Ben had told Lily he had the medical needs of the island

totally sorted—which wasn't quite true. He and Sam were both working full time and they never reached the end of the queue.

'Do you think these people have been saving their dramas for the last forty years, just waiting for us to arrive?' Sam asked a week after Lily had left. 'I thought medicine in a war zone was hard. This is ridiculous.'

'There is a financial issue,' Ben said thoughtfully. He'd talked to Gualberto at length now, and he had a clear idea of the problems Lily was facing. 'When Lily first started here there was no money for decent medical facilities. No one's looked at the broader picture since they found oil.'

'Lily won't have had time to look. She'll have been too busy to think past the next case of coral poisoning.' Sam lifted his day sheet, summarising his daily patients, and winced. 'Do you have any idea—?'

'How many times islanders cut themselves on coral and get infected? Yes,' Ben said. 'I saw six cases yesterday myself.'

'Maybe we could bomb the hell out of the coral,' Sam said morosely. 'That'd fix it.'

'There speaks a surgeon. If it hurts, chop it out.'

'You got any better ideas?'

'I have, actually,' Ben said. 'Use some of the oil money. Set up a first-rate health system, with a state-of-the-art hospital and medical bases on all outlying islands. We could advertise to medics from Australia initially but we need to organise more of the island kids into medical training. Lily was an exception—there's been none since. We need island kids thinking about medicine and ancillary services as careers. We also need a helicopter service devoted to medical needs, and staff to run it.'

'So…' Sam was regarding his friend in awe. 'A complete medical service for all the islands. This sounds serious. You're seriously thinking of setting this up?'

'Not me. But I can advise.'

'You wouldn't be tempted to stay?'

'It's not what I do.'

'You need to establish some sort of relationship with Benjy.'

'I'll see him at the farm when I leave here.'

'For a few days, on your way to the next disaster.'

'That's what I do.'

'Yeah,' Sam said, still thoughtful. 'So it is. I forgot.'

'Just as well I haven't,' Ben said, but as he walked away his friend's eyes stayed on him.

Thoughtful.

Life had slowed to a crawl. The biggest excitement was the impending arrival of Flicker's foal and after three weeks at the farm Lily was having trouble even sharing that.

She slept long and deeply, untroubled by dreams or nightmares. Benjy slept in the big bed beside her and after the first few days his dreams also seemed to disappear. He had needed this, Lily conceded. Ben had been right.

'We didn't need Jacques,' he confided to Lily, and Lily agreed.

'He wasn't a good man, Benjy.'

'I shouldn't have gone to him,' Benjy whispered. It was late at night and he was cuddled against her before sleep—a time when demons could be faced together and dispersed as unimportant.

'When Kira was killed I was really scared,' he whispered. 'I was running toward the beach and I heard shooting. Men were running up the road toward me so I ducked into the trees until they were past. Then I saw what had happened on the beach. I started running back to you but then I saw Jacques yelling at the men, really angry, and they weren't shooting at him so I came out of the trees and he said come with him.'

He snuggled even closer, trembling. 'But I shouldn't have, Mama.' He hesitated and then he added, 'Ben's nicer than Jacques.'

It wouldn't take a lot to be nicer than Jacques, Lily thought bitterly, but she made herself answer mildly. 'He is.'

'Is Ben our friend?'

'Yes.'

'Is he a better friend than Jacques?'

'He is,' Lily repeated, trying to figure what else to say. How to tell a child that Ben was much more than a friend? How to tell a child that a stranger was his father?

'He likes me better than Jacques did,' Benjy murmured.

'I went to university with Ben,' she told him. 'He's been my friend for a long time.'

'But he hasn't visited us before.'

'He's been busy, Benjy. He looks after everybody when there's trouble.'

'You look after everyone when they're in trouble.'

'No, but…' She hesitated. 'Benjy, on the island…when those men came…they were friends of Jacques and they wanted our oil. Jacques didn't know they were going to shoot anyone but they did. I think Jacques wanted to be rich. Ben doesn't want to be rich. He just wants to stop people hurting.'

'Like you.'

'A bit like me, but Ben travels all around the world. We stay on the island.'

'But you like it here,' Benjy reasoned. 'There might be lots of other places that are cool.'

'One place at a time,' she whispered, floundering.

'Doesn't Ben go to one place at a time?'

'I guess so.'

'Then he could still be our friend. We could visit him.'

'He goes to dangerous places.'

'Then he could keep visiting us,' Benjy persisted. 'We could tell him our place is dangerous and he would come then. It is dangerous.'

'It was only dangerous once. It's safe now. You know that.'

'Then he won't come and visit?'

'I don't know, sweetheart,' she said helplessly. 'Let's just wait and see.'

'She's only agreed to take four weeks off. If you leave it any longer, you won't have any time with her at all.'

'Maybe that'd be for the best,' Ben said for the tenth time or more.

'But what about Benjy? He's your kid,' Sam said, letting his exasperation show. 'Doesn't he deserve a father?'

Sam talked so much that occasionally he said something sensible. Ben had almost managed to turn off. But that comment... It hit a nerve.

Benjy deserved a father? He hadn't thought of it like that.

Until now he'd thought of this from his own point of view and from Lily's. Not from Benjy's.

'You can get by without one,' he said, trying to sound confident.

'Says you,' Sam said mockingly. 'Says the man whose parents tossed you into boarding school at five and paid people to look after you on holidays. You survived, so Benjy should, too? Is that what you think?'

'Where the hell do you get your information?'

'I'm a doctor,' Sam said smugly. 'We learn by listening in medical school. Plus I looked up your army notes. When you applied to this unit they gave you a psych test. As a medical officer I just happened to look...'

'You could get struck off for that.'

'I never look at anything that's not available from other sources if I had time to look,' Sam said virtuously. 'I'm just being time-efficient. But the psych test said you were a loner and listed your background as evidence. Hence you get the frontline work, while good old Sam, who has his Christmas with thirty or so relatives, gets to stay home till you clear up the villains.'

'So quit asking questions,' Ben growled. 'Use those sources of yours to find out what you want.'

'Med school taught me to get patient profiles from a variety of sources,' Sam said, still virtuous. 'The best source of all is the patient.'

'I'm not your patient.' His patience at an end, Ben's voice was practically a roar. They were in the staff quarters of the field hospital. The walls were canvas. There was a startled murmur from outside and Sam grinned.

'Great,' he said. 'That's started a bunch of rumours. Doctor cracks under pressure. You need a break. A nice family holiday?'

'Will you cut it out?'

'I'm playing family counsellor,' Sam said. 'It's my new role, starting now. Go make friends with your son and get yourself reattached to Lily.'

'You're single,' Ben snapped. 'Go find yourself a family.'

'Ah, but there's the rub,' Sam told him. 'You're not happily single. Me, I'm meeting ladies, shortening my list, figuring out where I fit in before I settle down. But you... You're running in fear, my friend. And I also got to know Benjy. He's a great kid and he deserves more than you're prepared to give. So I reckon you should reconsider. You're not needed here any more. You've set up the bones of the new medical service. We can do the rest. There's a chopper leaving in the morning. You should be on it.'

'Butt out.'

'Not until you're on the chopper.' Sam eyed him, consideringly. 'There's levels of brave, Lt Blayden,' Sam said softly. 'Off you go and face the next level.'

* * *

'Do you think Ben will come while you're here?' Rosa asked, and Benjy looked worried.

'We want him to come, don't we, Mama?'

'Mmm.' Lily tried to be noncommittal. They were walking back to the house, leading Flicker. The mare was growing heavier every day with the weight of her foal. She loved the lush pasture by the river but she couldn't be trusted to graze there by herself.

'Her normal paddock's on the far side of the river,' Rosa had explained. 'With the dry weather, the river's dropped and the ground on this side is marshy. If we left her be she'd end up stuck in mud.'

Lily wasn't sure if that was true, or it was an explanation designed so she and Benjy had to spend a couple of hours each morning supervising Flicker's grazing, but, contrivance or not, it was working. There was a lot to be said for supervising a pregnant mare and doing nothing else. This place was the Ben Blayden cure for post-traumatic stress.

Or the Ben Blayden heart cure?

No. His prescription hadn't worked for that.

'He's very busy,' she told Benjy. 'He's probably needed somewhere else by now.'

'There's time if you make time,' Rosa said darkly. She shook her head. 'He's so unhappy. Since he was a little boy he's been looking for a family.'

'Rosa…'

'I know.' Rosa smiled down at Benjy. 'I have big ideas for your mama and our Ben. But big ideas are not necessarily bad ideas. I just wish that he'd come.'

And two hours later he did. They were washing for lunch when they heard the helicopter, and Benjy was out of the house in a flash.

'It's got to be him,' he told Lily as she joined him on the veranda. 'It has to be.'

And it was.

CHAPTER NINE

BEN stepped out from under the rotor blades and looked across at the house. She was there.

Lily was standing on the veranda, dressed simply in shorts and a singlet top. Even from here she looked different.

And Benjy… Benjy was racing to meet him, a nugget of a kid, all arms and legs, his grin the same as Lily's, multiplied by ten.

His grin was Lily's grin before she'd taken on the worries of the world.

'Ben, Ben, Ben!' Ben was forced to drop his holdall as Benjy catapulted himself into his arms. Before he knew what was happening he was hugging his son and being hugged, and looking over the mop of curls to where Lily was smiling a welcome of her own. His gut twisted so sharply it was physical pain.

'Ben's here,' Benjy called, deeply satisfied, and wriggled in Ben's arms to face his mother.

'Really,' Lily said. 'I thought it was the milkman.'

'Silly,' Benjy said reprovingly. 'It's our Ben.'

'You never said that about Jacques.' Lily halted on the third step down from the veranda. Ben had reached the base of the steps. He needed to climb three steps to reach her but he hesitated, aware that this moment was important.

'I didn't like Jacques,' Benjy said, and buried his face in Ben's shoulder. 'He kept saying I had to be a man.'

'You're a kid,' Lily said.

'I know,' Benjy said, and peeped his mother a smile. The smile was pure mischief, Ben thought. He'd never seen Benjy like this, as free as kids were supposed to be free.

Their stay here had done them both worlds of good. He could read it in their faces.

Maybe they'd want to leave almost straight away.

Well, that was OK. He'd only dropped in to check on his way to the next mission. On his way to the next danger.

'I can ride a horse,' Benjy told him, wriggling until Ben set him on his feet. 'But not Flicker 'cos she's going to have a baby. Rosa says I can help choose a name for her foal.'

'And what about your mama?' Ben said, smiling up at Lily. 'Can she help choose?'

'Mama chose my name,' Benjy said. 'It's not fair that she chooses the horse's name, too.' He skipped up the steps to Lily. 'Why did you call me Ben's name?' he asked.

'Because…' Lily said, and faltered. She looked at Ben, in her eyes a question. Now or never, her gaze said, and he had to make an instant decision.

OK. He could do this. Maybe this wasn't the best time, but was there ever a good time for something so momentous? He nodded.

'Benjy, I've told you about Ben,' Lily said softly. 'I told you all about the good things he does and the brave doctor he is. What I should have told you, Benjy, is that Ben is your father.'

Ben's small mouth dropped open. He stared at his mother like she'd lost her mind. Then, very slowly, he turned on the steps to stare at Ben.

'You're my dad?'

'Yes,' Ben said, feeling…odd. 'I am.'

'Henri said Jacques would be my father.'

'No,' Lily said. 'Ben is.'

'You mean he gave you the tadpole that went into your egg,' Benjy demanded, and Ben almost choked, but he didn't because, funny or not, this was a really serious moment.

'That's it,' Lily said, sounding relieved.

'I knew I had to have a father somewhere,' Benjy said. He looked Ben up and down, head to toe. 'You're sure?'

'We're sure,' Ben said softly. 'We should have told you before, but I've been off adventuring and your mama didn't want to tell you by herself.'

Benjy considered that for all of ten seconds. He looked at it dispassionately—and decided it was acceptable. More than acceptable. His grin came back with a vengeance. 'Cool! Can I ring up Henri in hospital and tell him?'

'Sure,' Lily said. 'We'll ring tonight.'

'Can I tell Flicker now?'

'Of course.'

'Cool,' he said again, and breathed a great sigh of satisfaction. Then he bounced down the steps and headed horsewards to spread the news.

'I guess I've done what I came to do,' Ben managed. Benjy's departure had created a silence that was lasting too long. He didn't know how to break it and his words now sounded flippant. And sort of…final?

That was how she took it, anyway. 'You should have held the helicopter,' she said stiffly. 'Maybe if you radio fast they'll come back and collect you.'

That was so ridiculous that he didn't respond and she didn't press it.

'Tadpole, huh?' he ventured, and the tension eased a little. She managed a smile.

'Fathers are supposed to give their sons sex education. Not

mothers.' Her smile grew rueful. 'Actually, I didn't give him the tadpole bit. I suspect that was from Henri or another of his mates on the island.'

'Maybe it's time I took a hand.'

'If you have a better sex spiel than tadpoles, be my guest.'

Her agreement took him unawares. Here he was, meeting his son as his son for the first time, and Lily was handing over responsibility for sex education. It was his responsibility?

Maybe it was.

He wasn't going to be there.

'There's no need to panic,' Lily said, and he sensed a fraction of withdrawal of friendliness. 'I can do it myself.'

'I'd like to help.'

'I don't want help,' she said. 'Parenting's not about help. You either do it or you don't. You parent on your own terms.'

'That sounds ominous.'

'I read it in a book,' she confided, and suddenly she smiled again, abandoning tension. 'In truth I know nothing about the rules from here on in. You and Benjy will have to work it out for yourselves. But meanwhile Rosa and Doug will be aching to see you. They'll be trying to give us private time but just about busting a corpuscle to see you.'

'Busting a corpuscle?'

'It's a medical term,' she said wisely. 'I'm surprised you haven't heard of it. It involves mess into the middle of next week.'

He'd forgotten that. He'd forgotten Lily happy. He grinned at her; she grinned back and then she stood aside so he could come up the steps and past her into the house.

'Welcome home,' she murmured as he passed, and it was all he could do not to turn and kiss her. Maybe she would have welcomed it, he thought, but it behoved a man to act cautiously.

Nevertheless, as he passed her he was extremely glad that he hadn't asked the helicopter to wait.

* * *

They had a great dinner. Doug had pulled out all stops to create a feast. Roast beef with all the trimmings, followed by an apple pie that made Ben's eyes light up with pleasure the minute he saw it.

'I remember this pie.' He glanced at Doug and frowned. 'Hang on. When I was a kid here, you and Rosa worked outside. How did you know I loved this? How did you get the recipe?'

'Mrs Amson was the cook here then,' Doug said placidly. 'When you offered us the job I rang her and asked her for recipes.'

'For anything you liked,' Rosa said softly. 'It seemed the least we could do when you were handing us our lives back.'

Ben coloured. Lily stared across the table, fascinated. The normally in-control doctor who handled crisis after crisis with aplomb was seriously discombobulated.

'Why are you staring at Ben?' Benjy asked, her and Lily answered without thinking.

'He's discombobulated.'

Benjy thought about that for a minute and then giggled. 'That sounds like his arms and legs have come off.'

'Just his cool,' she said, and smiled across the table at Ben. 'I like to see a man discombobulated for good reason.'

'What's good reason?' Benjy asked, still intrigued.

'Because he does good things for people,' Rosa said, rising and starting to clear away. 'Except no one's supposed to thank him. He doesn't like people hugging him, our Ben, so all we can do is make him apple pie.'

'We could hug him,' Benjy said.

'So we could,' Lily agreed. 'He's been very good to us, our Ben.'

'He is our Ben,' Benjy agreed. He turned to Doug. 'He's my dad.'

'I thought that must be it,' Doug said gravely. 'And dads should be hugged.'

'I don't know whether he wants to be hugged.'

'You'll have to ask him.'

'Ask me tomorrow,' Ben said, getting up from the table in such a hurry that his chair crashed to the floor behind him. 'I need to take a walk.'

'We can come with you,' Benjy offered. 'Do you want to meet Flicker?'

'Tomorrow,' Ben said, backing out the door as if propelled. 'For now I need some space to myself.'

'He always needs space to himself.' Rosa and Lily were washing up. Benjy had asked Doug if he could do bedtime reading duty and Ben was nowhere to be seen. 'It'll take an indomitable lady to break down those barriers.'

'I'm not sure I'm that lady,' Lily said. She hesitated but by now she was sure Rosa had figured out everything there was to know about her, and she surely knew Ben as well. 'I'm not sure there'll ever be a lady for Ben.'

'He's looking like a man in love tonight.'

'He's looking like a man who's afraid.'

'If he asked you to marry him…'

'He won't,' Lily whispered. 'And even if he did, I can't leave the island.'

'Can't you?' Rosa dried her hands on the dishcloth and turned to face her. 'Is there really no one who could take your job?'

'There's no money to pay anyone.'

'Of course there is,' she said briskly. 'Doug and I have been reading the newspapers. Kapua has as much oil wealth as it wants. They can easily pay medical staff enough to encourage them to come. It's not like Kapua's a desert either. It sounds lovely.'

'It is lovely,' Lily whispered. 'It's home.'

'Home's where the heart is,' Rosa retorted. 'Look at me. I've been following Doug for years, working where he's needed to be.'

'But that's different.'

'Why is it different?'

'Because Ben wouldn't want us where he is. Nothing's changed since medical school. Like leaving the table now. The conversation was too close to the bone. He's cultivated armour and no one's getting through.'

'You love him,' Rosa said gently, and Lily nodded.

'I always have.'

'Then…'

'Then nothing,' she said. 'His armour's thirty years deep. No one's getting through. We'll stay in touch now for Benjy's sake, but we won't do more than that. And me? I have to rebuild some armour of my own.'

Which was why she should be in bed. Which was why she should be anywhere but where she was at midnight, which was sitting on the back veranda, waiting for Ben to come home.

He did come home, walking steadily across the paddocks in the moonlight. He was still wearing the army camouflages he'd been wearing when he'd arrived. Maybe he had no casual clothes here, she thought. These must be the only clothes he took with him as he travelled the world.

Or maybe there was a reason he still wore them. This was army camouflage, a reminder that he was still on duty somehow. A reminder that his armour had to stay.

He didn't see her as he strode up through the garden to the veranda. She was sitting on an ancient settee to one side of the front door.

'Have you been up to the peak?' she asked gently as he reached the top of the stairs, and he froze. There was a moment's stillness while he collected his thoughts. When he turned to her he was smiling but she wasn't sure the smile was real.

'You guessed.'

'It's a great place,' she told him. 'It made me stop.'

'Stop?'

'Let go,' she said gently. 'I spent the first few days here doing what I normally do—trying to cram in as much as I possibly could. Blair's Peak sort of took that out of me. I've slowed down so much now that I'm practically going backwards.'

'I'm glad. It's what you needed.'

'How about you?' she asked. 'Has it slowed you down?'

'Unlike you, I don't need to be slowed down. I'm not a workaholic.'

'Sam said you're an adrenalin junkie. Which is just as bad as me.'

'Sam doesn't know what he's talking about.'

'He's your friend.'

'I don't have friends.'

There was a silence at that. It stretched out into the night sky. Permeating everything.

'We were friends,' she said at last.

'And now I find you've borne me a son without telling me. So much for friendship.'

'You think it might have been something more, then?' she demanded. He was standing before her, dressed for battle, and that was suddenly how she was feeling. Like she was geared up for battle as well. She hesitated, but the look on his face said he wasn't even going to consider their relationship. OK, then, try another track. 'Do you love Rosa and Doug?' she asked, and his brows snapped down in confusion.

'What sort of question is that?'

'Just answer it. Do you?'

'As much as I love anyone.'

'That's what I thought. Do you know Doug has angina? Or worse. Rosa's terrified but she can't persuade him to go near a doctor.'

'Why didn't she say?'

'How can she say anything when your visits are so rare they make special dinners? They'd never dream of interrupting one of your visits with medical necessity.'

'That's crazy.'

'It is,' she retorted. 'It's because they love you.'

'Hell, Lily…'

'I'm tired,' she said, pushing herself to her feet. 'I wanted you to know about Doug, so if you leave tomorrow you'll at least know there's trouble here. He won't take advice from me. It sounds like angina but it could be more serious. I can't tell that unless I examine him and how can I?'

'I'll talk to him.'

'Which will solve the problem this time. But after that?'

'Hell, Lily, I'm not responsible for these people.'

'Then you should be,' she snapped. 'They love you. Just like…' She caught herself, drawing herself back, closing her mouth with a gasp. 'No. That's it. Leave it.'

'Lily—'

'Leave it!'

'Fine,' he said cautiously, and she made to push past him to go indoors. But his hand caught her shoulder and he turned her so she was facing him.

'Lily, you don't need to go back to the island.'

'Of course I need to go back to the island.'

'You don't,' he said heavily. 'Sam and I have worked it through with Gualberto. We've set up an embryonic medical service that should be up and running within weeks.'

'An embryonic medical service…'

'Gualberto's agreed,' he told her, eager to move to a neutral, impersonal topic. 'It's time for the island to stop sitting on all its resources. We had a massive meeting last week. The consensus is that they'll not exploit their oil for individual wealth but they'll spend real money on education and medicine. Which is where you come in.'

'I come in where?'

'Everyone knows you're overworked. The plan is to get at least two fully trained doctors plus interns working on the island—but that's just for starters. We see a medical service that eventually serves all outlying islands, with you or someone like you as administrator, but with every specialty represented. We see a much bigger hospital. You need connections to Australian teaching schools so Kapua can become part of their remote training roster for young doctors. You need a helicopter service for outlying islands, and the oil money is more than enough to fund it for generations to come. It'll be huge, Lily.'

She stared at him, dumbfounded, and ran her tongue over lips that were suddenly dry. 'You've set all this up already.'

'Yes. Gualberto—'

'Gualberto never thought of this by himself.'

'No. Sam and I—'

'Have been on the island for little more than a month,' she said blankly. 'What do you know about what we need?'

'We know what you need. Lily, this leaves you free to spend time away from the island.'

'Why would I spend time away from the island?'

'You could spend time with me,' he said, suddenly uncertain. 'Maybe we could spend a couple of weeks here a year. While I get to know Benjy.'

'You'll be a father two weeks a year?'

'I can hardly do more.'

'No,' she said bleakly. 'Of course you can't.'

'Lily, I don't do family.'

'Why the hell not?'

'I told you—'

'So many years ago. When we were kids. I'd hoped you'd change by now.'

He stared at her in the moonlight. 'What more do want of me, Lily?' he asked. 'You tell me.'

'I don't know,' she said wearily. 'But I'm scared. Benjy knows you're his dad, so now there's two of us. Two of us spending months of every year not knowing where you are. What you're doing. If Benjy get as attached to you as I am, how can I put him through that?'

'You're attached…'

'Of course I'm attached.' She sighed, 'You know I am. I tried so hard to fall in love with Jacques—with anyone—but all I ever wanted was you. You've been in my heart every minute since the day I met you. But I'm not letting you destroy my life. I'm not letting you mess with Benjy's life. Come here two weeks every year and fall in love with you all over again… How can I do that and survive?'

'Lily, it's what I am. It's non-negotiable. I didn't ask to be Benjy's father.'

'But that's non-negotiable, too.' She gulped for breath and regrouped. 'I didn't ask to be Benjy's mother, but I am. I didn't ask to fall in love with you, but I did. Ben, you've spent your entire life finding yourself a place where you didn't have to get attached. You swing into a crisis situation, save lives, do good but you never visit them again. You never need to hear feedback from patients two years after the event. You don't need to attach yourself to a community in any shape or form. Sam says you even hold yourself aloof from the crisis response team.'

'I can't help what I am.'

'No, and neither can I,' she said. 'But seeing you for two weeks every year… It'd destroy me, Ben. So somehow you need to work out a relationship with Benjy that doesn't include me, and don't ask me how you can do that because I don't know.

I'll support whatever you want but I can't continue to be near you. I just…can't.'

'Lily…'

'What?' She sighed again and looked up into his face. Which was a mistake.

Because, regardless of anything else, this was Ben. Her Ben. The Ben she'd carried in her heart for all these years.

He wasn't hers. She'd known that then and she knew it now. The scars of his childhood were too deeply etched. There was no place she could reach him.

'I'm sorry, Ben,' she whispered, and she reached up and touched his lips fleetingly with hers.

Which was a further mistake.

She backed away but as she did so she saw his eyes widen, flare.

'Lily,' he said, and it was the way he'd always said it. Like it was a caress.

'Lily.' It was a plea.

She didn't move. She didn't move and she didn't see him move, but she had or he had or whatever, and suddenly she was being held tightly in his arms, crushed against his chest, kissed and kissed some more.

This was dumb. This was crazy, letting herself be kissed in the moonlight, letting herself be kissed as she'd been kissed all those years ago.

For it was the same, exactly as she remembered. It was a searing, molten kiss that felt like two forces were being hauled together and fused into one. It was a white-hot heat that made her heart twist with longing and desire and love.

Ben.

She couldn't pull away. Where was the strength for that? Nowhere.

How could she ever have thought she could love Jacques? She'd tried so hard and she'd failed and she knew it was no character flaw in Jacques that had prevented it—though, heaven knew, it should have been. It was because she considered herself irrevocably married to this man.

Her heart.

But here was no happy ending. Ben had been raised to never give his heart. How could such a man change? How could such a man admit a need?

He couldn't, but she did. Oh, she did, she thought as her body melted into his. She kissed him back with a fierceness that matched his own. She loved him with every fibre of her being, willing him to soften, willing him to love her as she loved him.

His hands were tugging her against him. He felt wonderful—a big man, superbly muscled, strengthened by years of military training, moving from emergency to emergency, running…

He was still running, she thought in that tiny fragment of her mind that was available for such thought—which wasn't much, admittedly, but it was enough to tinge this kiss with sadness, to tinge it with the inevitability of parting.

He was so right for her. She was so right for him. Her breasts moulded against his chest as if she was somehow meant to be there. They'd been made in one cast and then split somehow, and now, for this tiny fragment of time, the two halves of the whole had come together.

There had to be a way. There had to.

The kiss extended for as long as a kiss could without moving to the next step—the seemingly inevitable step for a man and a woman who'd loved before and who'd been apart for seven long years. She couldn't take that step, she thought. She mustn't. There was no such thing as a one hundred per cent effective birth control and to take another pregnancy back to the island…

'No,' she managed as he drew back a little, and she saw a trace of confusion cross his face.

'No?'

Heaven knew where she found the strength to say it, but it had to be said. 'No further, Ben. We can't.'

'But—'

'I don't want another child.' But that was a lie, she thought. She'd love another child. Another piece of Ben to carry forward into her life without him.

'Hey, we're not about to…'

'We might have been about to,' she whispered. 'But we can't.'

'That doesn't make sense.'

'I think it does,' she said, and pulled further away. Just a little. Just as much as she could bear to. 'Ben, I love you.'

'Maybe I do—'

'Don't say it,' she said, suddenly urgent. 'Because you don't. You never have. You just love the part of me that you're prepared to accept.'

'What does that mean?' He seemed genuinely baffled and she shook her head. Nothing had changed, she thought bitterly. This was the same problem they'd had seven years ago. Oh, maybe it had been clearer then. The islanders had paid for her medical training and there was no way she could refuse to return. But there were two reasons she couldn't be near with Ben. One was her obligation to her island home. And the other was that Ben didn't want her.

Ben didn't want her.

'Maybe we could work something out,' he said, his voice husky with passion and desire. 'Lily, OK, I don't do family, but maybe… What I feel for you… There'll never be another woman I feel this way about. So maybe we could do something. Marriage or something. Maybe I could come to the island whenever I'm on leave.'

She stared at him, stunned. 'You're talking marriage?'

'I don't know.' He ran his fingers through his hair in a gesture of pure bewilderment. 'But we have to do something—to make this work.'

'For Benjy?'

'How can I be a father to him if you're not there? And if we were married, would that make you feel better about me being there—sometimes?'

'You're asking me to marry you because of Benjy?'

'I want you, too, Lily.'

'Two weeks a year?'

'However long I can spare. I'll try—'

'You can't just…try.'

But then she looked into his eyes and saw his confusion and she felt her heart twist. He was trying. He was trying so hard…

This was her Ben. If she said yes he'd sweep her into bed right now, she thought, and that was what she wanted more than anything else in the world. All she had to do was say yes and he'd marry her and Benjy would have a father and then…

And then he'd leave for the next crisis.

'Would you think of us while you were away?' she asked, and the look of surprise she saw in his eyes answered her question before he spoke.

'Of course I would,' he said, but she didn't believe him.

'Did you remember I was on Kapua?'

'Yes.'

'Sam said you didn't.'

'Sam—'

'Sam talks too much,' she whispered. 'But he answered my questions. He knows you well, Sam. And so do Doug and Rosa. They say you never stay long enough anywhere to be involved. You run like you're terrified of what happens if you lose your heart.'

'Psychoanalysis by Rosa and Doug.'

'And by Sam and by Lily,' she whispered. 'What did they do to you, those parents of yours, to make you so fearful?' She hesitated. 'Ben, what happened to Bethany?'

'Bethany…'

'Your sister. All the time we spent together, you never told me you had a sister.'

'She died when I was six. It's old news.'

'Did you love her?'

'Hell, Lily, I was tiny.'

'Did you love her?'

'That is none of your business. And it's nothing to do with what I am now. I'm a grown man.'

'Yes, you are.' She took a deep breath. 'And I'm a grown woman. A woman who thought about you every day that we were apart. Who'd die a little if you died. And who feels sick that you lost someone you loved and you won't talk about it. But you won't. You've closed off. God knows if it's because of your sister. I don't. You won't let me near enough to find out. But, Ben, if any of us went missing…Doug or Rosa or me or Benjy or Sam or anyone else who cares for you…would you miss us?'

'Of course.'

'Be truthful, Ben.'

He paused. She stepped back a little. The veranda light was on and she could see his face clearly. What she saw there answered her question without him finding the words.

'You'll never let yourself get that close,' she whispered. 'Will you?'

'Lily, I'm saying I think I love you.' He sounded exasperated rather than passionate, she thought. He sounded… confused? 'I'm offering marriage.'

She shook her head. 'How can you say you think you love me? Don't you know?'

'How can I know?'

'I'll tell you,' she said, anger coming to her aid. 'Love's great, but it's opening yourself again to that chasm of loss. It's lots else besides, but it's definitely not putting a signature on a piece of paper and a deal to spend a few days each year together.'

'I can't—'

'Of course you can't,' she said, anger fading and a bleak acceptance taking its place. 'Of course you can't. I should never have agreed to come here. I'm putting more pressure on you than you can bear. Even by telling you that Benjy is your son…'

'You should have.'

'If I had, maybe the pressure would have been on you for the last seven years and maybe you would have fallen properly in love. Or maybe you would have cracked under the strain. I don't know. But I do know that I need to back off now. I need to let you be.

'I'm going to bed now, Ben,' she said, and somehow she kept her voice resolute. 'I'm going to bed alone and I'll stay that way. Because no marriage at all is better than the one you're offering. I have to stay sane, for Benjy's sake if not my own.'

'Lily—'

'If I were you, I'd take another walk up to Blair Peak,' she told him. 'I think you need it more than I do. Oh, and, Ben…'

'Yes?' It was a clipped response. He was angry, she thought, and she knew it was confusion that was causing the anger. He thought he was doing the right thing—the noble thing. And she was rejecting that absolutely.

How hurtful was that?

Practicalities. When in doubt, talk medicine.

'Ben, Rosa's really worried about Doug,' she told him, and somehow her voice was steady. And it worked. She'd deflected him, she thought, seeing the relief in his eyes. Medicine was the great escape. 'Don't worry about me,' she said. 'Don't worry about Benjy. We'll be fine. Worry instead about Doug, who isn't fine.'

She saw the confusion fade still more. She saw him clutch at medical need as if he was clutching a lifeline.

'How long has he had pain?'

'Rosa says for months, but he's admitting little and he won't see a doctor. Rosa says he's been waiting for you.'

'For me?' he demanded, startled. 'Why the hell? I'm not his doctor.'

'No,' she said softly. 'There's an attachment there that I don't think you're admitting either.' She hesitated. 'Rosa's scared it's worse than Doug's letting on. She thinks Doug might want to talk to you about caring for Rosa if…'

'He'd know I would.'

'You would what?'

'Look after Rosa. But I need to find out what's wrong.'

'You'll look after Rosa how? If anything happened to Doug, she could hardly stay here.'

'This is a dumb conversation. Nothing's happening to Doug.'

'He's showing every sign of worrying himself into a coronary. Sure, he needs an examination and maybe treatment but the best thing you could do is what you're incapable of doing.'

'Which is?'

'Giving yourself,' she whispered. 'Telling Rosa you'll be here for her.'

'I'll look after her.'

'The same way you'd be husband and father to us? No,' she said sadly. 'That's no use to anyone. Oh, Ben.'

And she turned before he could say another word. She walked into the house and let the screen door slam behind her.

He did indeed walk up to Blair's Peak but the answers weren't there. She was asking too much of him, he told the night, but he knew that was a falsehood.

He was afraid.

She'd accused him of not loving. Of not throwing his heart into the ring and letting fate take a hand.

She was right.

Why?

He needed a shrink, he decided, but he sat up on the peak and he knew the answers were already his.

For the first time in more than twenty years he let himself think about Bethany.

At six he'd been sent to boarding school. Lots of kids were sent to boarding school at six. They survived, and he'd hardly seen anything of his parents anyway. He could hardly say he'd missed them.

But there'd been his kid sister. Bethany had been four years old to his six. His little sister. Even now the memories of her were warm and strong. With an assortment of nursery staff caring for them, Bethany had been his constant.

She'd suffered from asthma.

He still remembered the terror of her attacks. The feeling of helplessness as she'd gasped for breath. His six-year-old self telling untrained nursery staff what to do.

And then his father leaving him at boarding school. 'Who'll look after Bethany?' he'd demanded, and he could remember his desperation, the fear.

'She'll be looked after,' his father had said brusquely. 'You look after yourself.'

There had been nothing else to do. He'd looked after himself but Bethany had died before the year had ended. The school matron had told him of her death, her face crumpling with sympathy, moving to hug him, but he'd wanted none of it.

His parents hadn't come near him.

He looked after himself.

Any shrink in the world would tell him that was holding him back now. He knew it himself. But to break through…

He couldn't. He just…couldn't.

Even Blair Peak had no answers.

CHAPTER TEN

BREAKFAST the next morning was a strained affair. Once again Doug had gone to enormous trouble, frying home-cured bacon, making pancakes, setting the big kitchen table with fine china, old and fragile. Lily looked across at Doug's strained face. It was better than looking at the silent Ben, she thought, and there was enough tension on Doug's face to make her concerned. Why had he used the best china? The kitchen was equipped with a dishwasher but china like this would have to be hand-washed.

She concentrated on this small domestic problem rather than let herself think about Ben. Ben was eating silently, while Benjy was watching him with a certain degree of speculation. The knowledge that Ben was his father was clearly of immense importance to Benjy, and he was cautiously reassessing the man before him for parental qualities.

All in all, it didn't make for a casual breakfast.

Think about Doug, she told herself. Doug's eyes were as strained as Lily felt, and she wondered just how bad his chest pain was.

'Rosa and Benjy could take Flicker down to the river this morning,' she suggested. 'Ben and I will do the washing-up. You need to take a rest, Doug,' she told him with a sideways warning glance to Ben. 'You look as tired as I felt three weeks ago.'

But the elderly man was having none of it. 'Don't be daft, girl,' he said. 'You've lots of catching up to do, and if I know Ben he'll be flying out of here before we know it.'

'No, he won't,' Lily started, but then she looked uncertainly at Ben. 'Will you?'

'The chopper's not coming back till tomorrow,' Ben said. 'But if I need to, I can delay it.'

'That's what you call plenty of time,' Doug said derisively. 'To get to know your son. If that's all the time you have, there's no way I'm taking up any of it.'

'Doug, I'm really worried about your chest pain,' Lily said bluntly. If he really was hiding pain...

'I'm having no more pain now than I've been having for months. I read about it on the internet. It'll be angina. My mother had it for years and she died when she was ninety seven.' He managed a shaky grin. 'She was hit by a bus then, so that leaves me twenty odd years of angina before I meet my bus.'

'If it is angina,' Ben growled. 'We don't know. You need to be examined.'

'You can listen to my chest this afternoon,' Doug said, so much like he was conferring a benevolent favour that they all laughed. But even so... Lily's eyes met Ben's and she saw her concern reflected there.

Ben really did care, she thought. He tried desperately not to, but he couldn't hide it completely. Just as Doug couldn't hide the fact that he hurt.

Rosa rose and started clearing away plates, looking relieved. 'This afternoon you'll be examined, then,' she told Doug. 'You've agreed before witnesses so there's no wriggling out of it now. Meanwhile, I'll do the housework while Ben and Benjy and Lily take Flicker to the river. You rest. That's my final word, Doug, so no arguments.'

Doug opened his mouth to argue—but then thought better

of it and gave a sheepish grin. 'I can almost understand your reluctance to tie the knot,' he told Ben. 'See what you let yourself in for? Women!' He flung up his hands in surrender. 'Fine. I'll have an idle morning, as long as you three spend the morning together. Promise?'

'We promise,' Lily said. 'Don't we, Ben?'

'I'd rather examine you now,' Ben said, but Doug shook his head.

'That's an excuse not to spend time with Lily and Benjy, and you know it. I've had this discomfort for months and it's going nowhere. Stop your fussing and enjoy the day.'

So Ben, Lily and Benjy led the pregnant mare to the river. The day was fabulous, but Lily wasn't concentrating on the day. How could she ever break through this man's barriers? she wondered. And why wouldn't he talk about his sister? His silence hurt, but if it hurt her, how much more would it be hurting him?

'He's never talked about Bethany,' Rosa had told her. 'So I don't see how you can make him start now.'

They walked slowly. The mare was so heavy with foal that Ben was concerned. 'Are we sure we should be taking her out of the home paddock?'

'Rosa says a bit of exercise does her good,' Benjy told him. 'And she says the grass by the river is horse caviar.' He thought about that and frowned. 'I don't know what caviar is.'

'Fish eggs,' Ben told him, and Benjy wrinkled his nose in disbelief.

'So the grass tastes like fish eggs?'

'There's no accounting for taste,' Ben told him, and grinned. Benjy was leading the mare, with Ben by his side. Lily was walking behind, watching her son. And his father. The likeness was uncanny, she thought. The sun was glinting on two dark heads. Ben had only brought a small holdall with him, but he must leave clothes here for he'd finally ditched his uniform. This morning he was wearing chinos and an open-necked shirt with the sleeves rolled up. He looked wonderful, Lily thought, and the longing she had for him, the longing that had stayed with her for all those years, surged right back, as strong as ever.

She blinked back tears. She was right, she told herself fiercely. She couldn't marry this man. She couldn't break down the barriers. By herself she could block out this pain, but with the marriage he was suggesting it would stay with her all the time. She and Benjy would have a few short days with him, but then he'd be off, over and over, intent on his life of drama. Putting her and Benjy out of his mind. Not letting himself need…

There was the crux of the problem, she thought. She needed Ben, but he didn't need her. And he surely didn't need Benjy. He'd taught himself fiercely not to need, and who could blame him?

'Why do you like fighting?' Benjy asked him now, and she stilled and listened. They were trudging slowly toward the river, keeping pace with Flicker's slow amble. Ben and Benjy were at Flicker's head and Lily was behind, but Ben may as well have been talking to her.

'I don't like fighting,' he said. 'But when fighting happens, people are often wounded. That's what happened on your island. My job is to fix people after fighting. Or sometimes I go to where other bad things have happened, like tsunamis and earthquakes.'

'My mama fixes people,' Benjy said, following a line of reasoning yet to be disclosed.

'She does.'

'Are your people hurt worse than Mama's people?'

'I guess not. It depends.'

'And do you get to see the people when they're better? Mama says that's the best thing about doctoring. She sees people when they're sick and then one day when they're better they come to our house and sit on our porch and tell Mama how better they're feeling. Or the ladies come and show us their babies. Sometimes Mama even cries when she hugs the babies. Do you cry when you hug babies?'

'That's not what I do.'

'I guess mamas wouldn't come close to you with babies when you're wearing your scary uniform.'

'Maybe they wouldn't.' Ben sounded strained to breaking point, Lily thought. He wasn't enjoying this one bit. If the helicopter landed right now, would he climb aboard?

'I like you better without your uniform,' Benjy told him, giving a little skip of contentment, as if his line of questioning had achieved the results he'd wanted. 'But I need a picture of you in your uniform. Henri will think it's cool, but it's better like you are now. You're more like a real dad now.'

'Thanks.'

'Can you kick a football?'

'Yes.'

'Can you swim?'

'Yes.'

'Will you swim a race with me at the river?'

'I didn't bring my gear.'

'You can swim in your boxers,' Benjy told him. 'I swim in my boxers.' Then a thought occurred to him. 'Doug wears flappy white jocks that make me giggle when Rosa hangs them on the clothesline. But Henri's dad wears boxers. You don't wear flappy white things, do you?'

'Um…no.'

'Ace,' Benjy said, satisfied. 'Mama can hold Flicker and we'll go swimming.'

'Doesn't your mama go swimming?'

'Someone has to look after Flicker. She's the mama.'

'That's not very fair.'

'I'm happy to watch,' Lily volunteered from behind them. 'After all, Benjy can go swimming with his mama every day. How often can he go swimming with his dad?'

So she sat on the grassy bank, watching her son and his father swim, while Flicker grazed contentedly beside her.

Benjy swam like a little fish. Island kids practically swam before they could walk and Lily took it as a given, but she saw now that Ben was astounded by his small son's skill. This was no splashing-in-the-shallows swim. This was an exercise in Benjy showing his dad exactly what sort of kid he had. He weaved and ducked around Ben's legs, surfacing when least expected, doing handstands so his small feet were all that was seen above the water, challenging Ben to a race...

But Ben was a fine swimmer, too. They raced from one tree fallen by the river bank to another three hundred yards upstream. Lily watched as Ben started to race. She saw him check his pace and she knew he was holding back so Benjy could win.

She grinned—and she saw the exact moment when Ben realised Benjy had been checking his pace as well, but only so he could put on a burst of speed at the end. Benjy's small body surged ahead and suddenly Ben was left behind. His raw strength wasn't enough to compensate for the lead he'd given Benjy. Benjy surfaced, glowing, laughing at Ben and then calling triumphantly to his mother.

'He thought he had to give me a head start,' he yelled to Lily. 'So I won.'

'More fool him. Race again,' Lily decreed, so they did. This time Ben didn't hold back. He used all his strength and all his skill—and he only just won.

'You beat me,' Benjy said, growing happier by the minute. 'Mama can't beat me. A daddy should be able to beat his kid.'

'Then stop getting better,' Ben growled, but, watching him, Lily saw his sudden flash of pride.

And then shock.

Up until then fatherhood had been some sort of abstract concept, she thought. Sure, he'd been shocked to learn of Benjy's existence and then he'd been concerned about him, but this was something else. This child was his son—this little boy who had so much life ahead of him, who had so much potential to be proud of. Swimming was one tiny thing but there'd be so much more as he grew. Little and big. Lily watched as myriad emotions washed across Ben's face and she wondered how he was going to handle this.

She thought how she'd felt as Kira had handed over her newborn son to her six years ago, and she saw those same emotions reflected now on Ben's face.

'Now we can make sand bombs,' Benjy announced. 'Can you make sand bombs? Don't worry if you can't 'cos I'll teach you.'

It was a day of wonders. Benjy had a father, a father he could be proud of, and he intended to milk it for all it was worth.

'If you're leaving tomorrow, we have to hurry up,' he told Ben. 'I can teach you to fish. I'm a really good fisherman. Can you teach me to shoot with guns?'

That was a discordant note, but it didn't spoil the day.

'I'm a doctor, mate,' Ben told his son. 'I might wear army fatigues but I don't shoot.'

'You'd shoot if you had to?'

'I won't have to.'

Benjy thought about that and found it was acceptable. 'OK, then. Can you ride a horse?'

The only bad part of the day was the discussion that went on after Ben examined Doug. Doug managed to hold Ben off until late afternoon, but finally Ben told him if he didn't submit then he, Rosa, Lily and Benjy would subdue him by force. Doug didn't smile, which was a measure of how frightened he really was, Lily thought, and when Ben came out of the bedroom after the examination his face confirmed those fears.

'Hell, Rosa, how long has he had this level of pain?'

'I don't know.' Rosa bit her lip, looking suddenly old. 'Six months that he's admitted to me. Maybe longer. He only admitted it to me when I found him in the kitchen one night looking grey and sick. He said it was indigestion but I didn't believe him.'

'But you didn't insist he see a doctor.'

Rosa swallowed. 'Maybe I was afraid to,' she whispered. 'My dad died of a heart attack. To admit Doug has a bad heart… I just kept hoping you'd come home.'

They thought of Ben almost as their son, Lily thought. There was such a depth of emotion in Rosa's voice. *I just kept hoping you'd come home.*

And Ben heard it. She watched his face and there were was an echo there of the emotions he'd felt that morning. He had a son, and now he had something akin to parents.

And a wife?

He couldn't accept any of those things. She saw the tiny flare of panic behind his eyes and she thought there was no way he'd take this further. Parents, son, wife? The whole domestic catastrophe?

No.

'There's definite arrhythmia,' he told Rosa, and Lily knew that once again he was seeking some sort of refuge in medicine. His voice was brusque and strained. 'There's something badly wrong. His blood pressure's high as well. I'm guessing he's had some sort of infarct—a heart attack. Maybe that's what it was the night you said he was in such pain. He's telling me the pain's not so bad now, but he's still uncomfortable, which means the pain before must have been awful.'

'Dear God,' Rosa whispered, colour draining from her face. She clutched at Lily. 'You think…'

'Ben's not saying he's going to die,' Lily told her, guiding her into a chair by the stove. Benjy had gone to his bedroom to sort story books he wanted Ben to read to him that night, and she thanked God for it. The sight of Rosa's face would have terrified him.

'Rosa, how old was your dad when he died?' Ben asked softly, and Lily nodded, silently agreeing with his line of questioning. Let's get to the heart of the terror here.

'Fifty-three,' Rosa whispered. 'Almost twenty years younger than Doug is now. He had pain, just like Doug, and there wasn't anything we could do about it. One day his heart stopped, just like that. So I thought…when Doug started getting the pain…well, what can doctors do? That's why I didn't insist. He's better staying here for whatever time he has left.'

'There's lots doctors can do,' Ben told her, and Lily thought he really was a good doctor. Tensions forgotten, he was facing down terror with confidence and reassurance. 'You must have heard of bypass surgery.'

'Yes, but—'

'No buts,' Ben told her. 'I'm listening to Doug's heart and I'm hearing a heart under strain. I'm not a specialist and it'll take tests to find out exactly what's wrong, but I'm suspecting he has minor blockages. One or more of the blood vessels running to or from the heart have probably narrowed, to the point where the blood supply is compromised. Forty years ago there was nothing we could do. Now bypass surgery is so common it's done routinely in every major hospital. Lily will concur.'

'I concur,' Lily murmured.

'So all we need to do is get Doug to one of those hospitals.'

'He'll never agree.'

'He has agreed,' Ben said. Then he added ruefully, 'Though not as soon as I'd like.'

'How soon would you like?'

'Now,' Ben said promptly. 'With pain like his, he's a walking time bomb. But he's refusing to leave until I leave.'

'But you're not leaving until…'

'Tomorrow,' Ben said. 'There's a Medivac helicopter in the area tomorrow. It was tentatively due to collect me, but I'll radio them to pick us both up.'

And that will be that, Lily thought. He'd found an excuse to run.

'You shouldn't go yet,' Rosa whispered.

'I need to go. I was only intending to stay for a couple of days and I need to accompany Doug.'

Of course you do, Lily thought bitterly. The medical imperative.

'Can I come, too?' Rosa asked, and then she bit her lip. 'But I can't leave the farm. Flicker…'

'I'll organise for someone to fly in and take over,' Ben told her. 'It'll be twenty-four hours at most. Then we'll fly you out to join Doug.'

'It'll need to be someone who's good with horses.' Rosa was clearly torn. 'Flicker's due within the next week.'

'It'll be someone who's good with horses,' Ben assured her. 'You know I inherited three farms from my parents. I still keep them as working farms and I have excellent staff on each. I'll transfer someone here as soon as I can. When Doug's recovered we'll bring him back, and I'll leave someone here to help as long as you need.'

'Thank you,' Rosa whispered, her eyes suddenly brimming with tears. 'I think… Can I go and see Doug now?'

'Of course,' Ben told her. 'But he stays in bed and rests until we leave. If he doesn't then I call in a Medivac team right now.'

'That's fine by me,' Rosa whispered, and fled.

Which left the two of them, facing off over the kitchen table.

She should shut up, Lily thought dully. She should say nothing. There was nothing to be gained by conflict.

But she was going to have to tell Benjy that Ben was definitely leaving. The thought of his disappointment made her cringe.

'So there's no doctor on the Medivac chopper?'

'Sorry?'

'You know very well what I mean. I assume the chopper will be bringing someone back to this district from the city. Is that what you meant when you said it'd be in the area tomorrow?'

'Yes.'

'Since when has the Medivac service carried patients without a medical team?'

'I didn't ask.'

'You didn't ask whether there'd be a doctor on board?' She raised her brows in disbelief. 'Maybe we can ask now.'

'Doug wants me to go with him. He's terrified.'

'And so are you.'

'What are you talking about?'

'You're falling in love with your son,' she said softly. 'For you that's even more terrifying than falling in love with me. So you're running. The trouble is… I'll back off. I'm not sure Benjy will.'

'He'll be back on your island and I won't see him.'

It was a gut response. He said it and then realised what he'd said. It was an acknowledgement of fear. An acknowledgement that he was putting as much distance as possible between himself and his embryonic family.

'Coward,' Lily whispered.

'I'm not a coward.'

'Rosa told me about Bethany. How many years have I known you, Ben, yet you never told me about your sister? You've been running since then?'

'Rosa had no right. And I'm not running.'

'You know you are.'

'It's you who's refusing to marry me.'

'That's a joke. You don't know what marriage is. It's surely not waiting for you to drop in for a few days each year.'

'Lily—'

'Leave it,' she said dully. 'But don't pretend to be hurt because I won't marry you. You're not asking me to marry you. You don't know what the word means.'

They ate a desultory dinner—steak, cooked by Lily and not even close to the wonderful food Doug had prepared—and then Lily and Benjy went for a walk to say goodnight to Flicker, Rosa went to sit with Doug and Ben was left to his own devices.

He'd expected to spend that evening with Benjy. He'd thought maybe they could do something together—some sort of bonding thing, he thought, like taking a cricket bat and hitting a few balls. He only had tonight. He should be angry that Benjy had elected to go with his mother and talk to a horse rather than spend time with him.

But Benjy had watched him over the dining table and had made his own decision. Benjy had lost Kira only a few weeks ago. That pain would be still be raw. Maybe he wasn't going to put himself in the position where it hurt again.

Or maybe it already hurt. Ben had been there when Lily had told Benjy that Ben would be leaving in the morning. He'd seen his face shut down.

He knew that look. He'd perfected it himself.

So...

So stay, he told himself as he walked out onto the veranda. In front of the house was the home paddock. Benjy and Lily would be there with Flicker. He could join them.

But his feet turned the other way. He walked down to the beach, found a likely looking sand-hill and sat and watched the moon over the water.

Out there was Kapua. Home to Lily and Benjy.

He could get there twice a year, he thought, or maybe even more if he made the visits brief. Whenever he had a decent leave, he could spend a few days with Benjy.

But he had a night free now and Benjy had elected to go with his mother. As Lily had elected to stay with Benjy.

'We're all protecting ourselves,' he told the night.

He thought about the plan they'd made for the medical services for Kapua and the outlying islands. Lily could take over the role of medical director but there was another major position to be advertised. Director of Remote Medical Services—a doctor who'd be based in Kapua but who would take care of the outlying islands. He and Sam had listed the requirements for such a position. Emergency medicine. An ability to work alone. Experience in tropical medicine. And preference would be given to someone with a pilot's licence—someone who in an emergency could take control of a helicopter.

'Hey, I know someone who fits this,' Sam had said. 'Do you?'

Ben had ignored him. He'd had to. Because if he ever took a job like that, then every night he'd come home to Lily and Benjy.

So? Lily was quite simply the loveliest woman he'd ever met. Would ever meet. The way he felt about her was non-negotiable. And Benjy was great. Benjy was his son.

So why the terror? Why the ice-cold feeling that gripped his guts whenever he thought about taking things further?

Committing, not to a marriage but to a relationship where Benjy and Lily were permitted to need him.

Maybe he should just jump in at the deep end. Try it out and see.

But if he failed...

He'd looked at Lily's face tonight over the dinner table, and he'd looked at Benjy's, and he'd seen the same wooden look of pain. He'd hurt them already. How much more would he hurt them if he committed?

He wanted Lily to commit.

No, he didn't. He saw it now, more clearly than he'd seen it at any time in his life. Lily was prepared to throw her heart into the ring, and maybe so was Benjy, but didn't they understand that he could crush it? If he wasn't capable...

'Coward,' he told himself, but it didn't help a thing.

Lily lay in the dark and stared at the ceiling. She was under no illusions. Tomorrow Ben would leave. She'd see him next when he made a flying visit to Kapua to see his son.

So what was different? She'd lived with loneliness for seven long years.

But now she didn't even have Kira.

She hadn't wept for the old woman. She'd stood at the graveside and her face had stayed wooden. She'd felt wooden.

But now...

She wanted Kira and the pain she felt for the wonderful woman who'd been part of her life for so long was suddenly so acute she couldn't bear it. And it was mixed up with the way she felt about Ben. She'd loved and she'd lost.

She'd never admitted to herself that she hoped Ben might resurface in her life. She'd even finally agreed to marry Jacques. But maybe that thought had always been there—that tiny flare of hope.

And now it was dead. As Kira was dead.

Life went on. As a doctor she'd seen grief from many angles and she knew that grief could finally be set aside.

But not tonight. The house was asleep. Her son was asleep. She wasn't needed. There was no one to see her.

Dr Lily Cyprano buried her head in her pillow and she wept.

Breakfast the next morning was dreadful. None of them seemed to have appetites. Doug had refused to stay in bed but he was grim-faced and silent. He looked strained and ill, Lily thought, and even though it meant Ben would leave, she was relieved for Doug's sake. Doug needed specialist medical intervention urgently. She even found it in herself to be grateful Ben was going with him. That must give some reassurance to Rosa. Rosa trusted Ben implicitly.

Maybe she did, too.

'When will everyone be coming back?' Benjy asked in a small voice, pushing his toast away uneaten.

'Doug will be back here in a couple of weeks,' Lily told him. 'After the doctors have fixed him up.'

'What about my dad?'

They all waited for Ben to answer that, but he didn't. He concentrated on buttering his toast and Lily stopped thinking she trusted him implicitly and instead allowed anger to surge. She glowered across the table at Ben. Low life, she told herself, but it didn't work. She couldn't produce anger.

He wasn't someone she could be angry with, she thought miserably. He was just Ben. A man so wounded by life that he could never make a recovery.

'We'll be gone by the time Ben gets back,' she told Benjy gently. 'But he's promised to visit us on Kapua.'

That was something, but not enough. Benjy sniffed and

sniffed again, heroically holding back the tears Lily had shed the night before.

'Come out with me to see how Flicker is this morning,' Rosa suggested, rising from her own uneaten breakfast and casting an uncertain look at her husband. 'You're ready?'

'Bring on the chopper,' Doug said morosely. 'You've packed everything I could possibly need.'

'While you cleaned the kitchen,' she snapped. 'He got up at dawn and scrubbed out the cupboards,' she told Ben and Lily. 'Of all the obstinate, pig-headed...'

'Go out with the boy,' Doug said. 'Please, Rosa. You're making me nervous.'

'Fine,' Rosa muttered. There was still half an hour before the helicopter was due and she looked strained to the point of collapse.

'I'll check on the chopper time,' Ben said, and Lily knew he wanted the chopper to be there now. Just for Doug? Or was he running, too?

Of course he was running.

'Lily, I need to run through what has to be done here while we're away,' Doug told her, dragging his eyes from his wife's strained face. 'If you're to stay here until Ben sends help then I need to make a list.'

'Fine,' Lily told him. Rosa and Benjy went out one door. Ben went out the other. She stared at the closed door for a moment—and then turned back to Doug.

Doug had turned to the bench to find a pad and pencil. He lifted the pencil a couple of inches from the pad.

'Oh,' he said, in a tiny, startled voice, and he dropped the pencil.

'Doug?'

Nothing. She saw his eyes focus inward.

'Doug!'

By the time Lily reached him he was sliding lifelessly onto the floor.

'Ben,' Lily was screaming even as she broke Doug's fall. She lowered him to the floor, taking his weight. He'd slumped between a chair and the bench. She shoved the chair out of the way with her feet. It crashed into another and splintered.

She didn't notice.

Doug wasn't breathing. She had her fingers on his neck, frantically trying to find a pulse.

None.

'Ben,' she screamed again. She'd been three weeks away from medicine but she was all doctor now. She hauled Doug onto his back, ripping his shirt open.

'Ben!'

He'd heard. The door slammed open and Ben was with her, shoving the mess of furniture out of the way so savagely that the chair leg Lily had broken splintered off and skittered over the linoleum.

'Check his airway,' Lily snapped, and Ben was already doing it, feeling in Doug's mouth, turning his face to the side as Lily thumped down on his chest.

Ben stooped and breathed into Doug's mouth, then straightened. 'Let me,' he told Lily, and she knew at once what he meant. CPR needed strength and he had more of it than she did.

'Do we have any oxygen?' she demanded.

'No.' His hands were already striking Doug's chest, over and over, trying desperately to put pressure on his heart as Lily gave the next breath. 'Come on, Doug. Don't you dare die. Come on, Doug. Please. Come on.' His eyes didn't leave Doug's face as the CPR continued, strong and sure and as rhythmic as Lily could possibly want. 'Please.'

Please. Lily couldn't talk but she could pray, over and over. Please. She breathed and she waited and she breathed and she prayed and she breathed and prayed some more. There was a roaring overhead and it was the backdrop to her prayer, building in volume as she breathed and Ben swore and pushed downward over and over.

Please...

The door swung inward. 'Doug, it's the helicopter...'

It was Rosa. She took one step inside the door and stopped dead as she saw what was in front of her. Her hands flew to her face, her colour draining. 'Oh, God.'

'Rosa, is that the Medivac chopper?' Ben's voice was curt and hard, slicing across her terror.

'Doug—'

'Rosa, tell me.' His order was almost brutal. 'Is that the Medivac chopper? Yes or no?'

'Yes,' she whispered. Her face was as ashen as Doug's and she clutched for the table for support.

But Ben would have none of it. Terror was an indulgence they had no time for. 'Then run,' he told her. 'We need oxygen and a defibrillator. They'll have them on board. Run, Rosa. We'll save him yet.'

Rosa gave a gasp of sheer dread—and turned and ran.

There was no choice but to continue. Lily kept on breathing. She'd never done artificial respiration without an airway, but there was no hesitation. Doug felt like family.

It had to work.

Please.

Then...

At first she thought she was imagining it. It was the air she was breathing in for him that was making his chest rise.

But no. She drew back as Ben kept applying pressure, and she saw it again. Chest movement she wasn't causing.

'Ben,' she screamed and he drew back, just a little.

And she was right. Doug's chest rose imperceptibly, all by

itlsef. A weak shudder ran through his body and his eyes flickered.

Then Rosa waas back, bursting through the door with a man and a woman behind her. They were dressed in the uniforms of the Australian Medivac Service. Rosa must have been coherent enough to make herself heard, for the woman was carrying a medical bag and the man was carrying a defibrillator.

But maybe, blessedly, a defibrillator wouldn't be needed.

'Oxygen,' ben snpped, not taking his eyes off Doug. 'We have a pulse.'

Dear God...

One of the newcomers—the woman—was hauling open her medical bag. lily grabbed an oxygen mask and was fitting it to Doug's face before the girl could make a demur.

The man was carrying an oxygen cylinder as well as the defibrillator. he set it on the floor and Ben fitted it swiftly to the tube attached to Doug's mask. he watched Doug's chest every minute. As did they all. They had no attached monitor—all they could go by was the rise and fall of Doug's chest.

But it rose and it fell.

'Let's get an IV line up,' Ben snapped. The two newcomers ad obviously realised by now that Ben was a doctor—or maybe they already knew—and they'd merged seamlessly into a highly skilled team. There were now four medics and the right equipment, and suddenly Doug had a chance.

More than a chance. his eyes flickered open again and this time they stayed open.

'Don't try to talk,' Lily said urgently. 'Doug, you've had a heart attack, but you're OK. You'll be fine if you stay still.'

'Rosa.' He didn't say the word but Lily saw his lips move and knew what he wanted. She shifted a little so he could see his wife and Rosa could see him.

'She's here,' Lily said, and she felt like bursting into

tears—but, of course, she didn't because she was a doctor and doctors didn't weep over their patients, no matter how much they felt like it.

But she looked across Doug's body at Ben, and she saw exactly the same emotion on Ben's face as she was feeling herself.

Doctors didn't cry. No matter how much they wanted to.

And after all Ben's conniving, the choosing of who would leave the farm today was now decided differently.

The two Medivac officers were Dr Claire Tynall and Harry Hooper, a nurse trained in intensive care. Claire and Harry took over Doug's care with smooth efficiency, fitting a heart monitor, adjusting the oxygen supply, transferring Doug to a stretcher that could be raised onto wheels so he could be could be transferred easily to the chopper. There was space for one more person in the helicopter and it wasn't going to be Ben.

'I need to go with him,' Rosa sobbed, and Ben agreed.

'Of course you do. Lily, could you pack her some essentials while we get Doug into the chopper?'

So Lily did a fast grab from Rosa and Doug's residence while they loaded him. Doug was at risk of arresting again. They had to get him to a major cardiac unit fast.

'I hope this is all you need,' Lily told Rosa as she ran to the helicopter to find Doug and Rosa already aboard.

'Buy whatever else you need and put it down to me,' Ben said gruffly. 'I'll be with you as soon as I can.' Then, as Rosa's face crumpled in distress, he climbed up into the chopper and gave Rosa a swift hug.

That was it. Ben climbed down again. The door slammed shut. The chopper rose into the morning sky. It hung above their head for an instant, then headed inland.

Ben and Lily were left standing side by side, staring after it.

'It's OK, Lily,' Ben said, as if reassuring himself. 'We did good.' He reached out and touched her hand.

'We did, didn't we?' she said, and her voice broke. She pulled away—just a little but enough. It was suddenly enormously important that she didn't touch him. She was very close to complete disintegration. She'd seen deaths from cardiac arrest many times in her professional life, but today… Well, things had changed. She'd stayed independent, too, she thought, but Ben had come back to her and now her independence was a thing of the past.

But she had to find it again. She had to.

'He'll be OK,' Ben muttered, as the sound of he helicopter faded to nothing. He shoved his hands deep into his pockets and Lily thought he looked as strained as Rosa had.

He loved these people.

'He will be,' she said softly, in the voice she might have used for a frightened family member after a trauma. He looked… bewildered?

'I… Yes.'

He was more than bewildered. He was in shock, she thought, but she had to move on.

'I need to find Benjy,' she managed. 'Are you OK?'

'Of course I'm OK,' he said, and he seemed to give himself a mental shake. 'Why wouldn't I be?'

'Because someone you love almost died?'

'I don't…'

'Love? Yes, you do,' she whispered. She held his gaze for a moment, watching what looked like a struggle behind his eyes. Had he not realised how important Doug and Rosa were to him? They were desperately important, she thought, maybe in the same way Kira had been important to her.

The aching void of loss slammed home again, as it had hit home time and time again since Kira's death. But at least Kira had died knowing she was loved, Lily thought. At least she'd told the old lady that she was loved, and so had Benjy.

Had Ben ever told Rosa and Doug they were loved? Had he admitted it to himself?

'You'll see them soon,' she said softly, and he flinched.

'Sure.' He shook his head, somehow hauling himself back under some sort of control. 'I'll…I'll get someone here to take over the farm as soon as I can.'

Because you want to see Doug and Rosa, or because you want to leave us? Lily wondered, but she didn't say it. She had to do a bit of self-protection here, too.

'I…I need to find Benjy,' she repeated. She needed to give her little boy a hug—mostly because she needed a hug herself.

The totally in-control Ben Blayden seemed somehow now right out of his comfort zone. He was staring ahead like he was looking into an abyss. And maybe he was even considering jumping. 'OK,' he managed. 'Let's find…let's find our son.'

Our son? Lily thought. Our son? But he was already moving away. Questions had to wait.

CHAPTER ELEVEN

FINDING Benjy was easier said than done.

Despite the emotional nuances between Lily and Ben, almost as soon as she thought about Benjy Lily was aware of a wave of unease. Where was he?

As she hurried back to the house she forced herself to rewind the events of the last half-hour. Rosa and Benjy had gone out to talk to Flicker, but then Rosa had hurried back to tell them the helicopter was there. Benjy may well have stayed with Flicker.

But he must have seen the helicopter land, she thought. Wouldn't he have come back to the house by now?

Ben was by her side but before she reached the house she'd started to run, leaving him behind. 'Can you check the front of the house?' she called. She ran up the veranda steps, just inside the back door. 'Benjy?'

No Benjy.

OK, he must still be with Flicker. She walked back out onto the veranda, expecting to see Benjy on his favourite perch, on the end of the water trough where he talked to Flicker. In these last weeks Flicker had become Benjy's new best friend; someone to talk to when adults didn't cut it.

But the trough was bare. He *must* be in the house, Lily

thought, retracing her steps. Had he come in while they'd been trying to save Doug? What had he seen? Benjy had suffered too much trauma for one small boy.

She reached the back door again and started to call, but then she turned again to stare down at the home paddock.

She'd almost missed it. Her eyes had swept the paddock, looking for Benjy. But now… She did another long perusal. There were no other animals in the home paddock.

The other four horses were grazing in the pasture on the far side of the river. It was only Flicker who was kept this side, as Rosa wanted her close for foaling. But the gate at the far side of the paddock was open, and Flicker was gone.

She catapulted down the back steps. Ben came around the corner of the house and she almost ran into him.

'Whoa,' he said, reaching out and steadying her. 'He's not out the front. Isn't he here?'

'N-no,' she stammered. 'Neither is Flicker. The gate's open.'

Ben stilled. Without releasing Lily, he turned to check the paddock.

Nothing.

'Would he have tried to take her to the river?'

'Maybe he would,' Lily whispered. 'He was so upset about you going. If he and Rosa were getting Flicker ready for her daily walk and Rosa came back inside…'

'Let's go.'

Side by side they ran, down the track leading to the pasture where they normally brought the mare to graze. They reached the rocky outcrop at the bend to the horse pasture and stopped dead as they saw the deserted river bank before them.

No horse. No small boy.

'She's a strong horse,' Lily whispered. 'At the fork in the track even Rosa sometimes has a battle turning her this way. Rosa says she wants to join the other horses.'

'Closer to the sea,' Ben said, and they were already moving. 'Hell, it's marsh down there. If the horse gets stuck…'

And it seemed that was just what had happened.

For most of its length this river was deep and fast, surging from the mountains to form a swift-running channel, but at its mouth it broadened and shallowed.

On the far side of the river was a rocky incline, delineating the edge, but not this side. Because it was summer and the water from the mountain catchment was less, the width of river had narrowed. There was now thirty or forty yards of river-flat on this side, normally under water but now dry. Or almost dry.

On the far side of the river Lily saw the other four horses belonging to the property. They were staring over the river toward a clump of rocks. For a moment she couldn't see what they were staring at. And then, appallingly, she did.

Flicker was there, half-hidden by the rocks. Lily hadn't seen her because she'd been searching for something of horse height and Flicker was now a lot lower than horse height. The mare had taken herself halfway across the flat, trying to reach her companions. And then she'd sunk. She was up to her withers in mud, struggling to free herself from what looked to be an impossible situation.

Her world stilled. Where was Benjy? Dear God, where was Benjy?

But Ben was there before her. 'Benjy.' Ben was yelling his son's name, breaking into a run across the mud, regardless of whether it was safe or not. 'Benjy!'

'I'm here.' It was a terrified wail from behind the horse. 'Dad, I'm here. Help me.'

She was running almost as fast as Ben. The ground gave a little under her feet, but she was moving too fast to sink. It was firm enough to hold her—just—but it was a miracle Flicker had got this far out.

Ben reached the horse before she did. By the time she reached them he was around the other side of Flicker. And there was Benjy. He was still clutching the halter as if he alone could stop the mare sinking, but the mare's struggles had made the ground at her head a quagmire. It looked a glutinous mess that had hauled Benjy into it as well as the mare. He'd sunk to his chest, and the mare's struggles were driving them both deeper.

But Ben had him. He sat on the ground behind Benjy, with his legs on either side of his son. His arms came around Benjy's chest, and he leaned backward.

'Don't struggle,' he told Benjy. 'Just go limp in my arms. Let me do the work.' He looked at the mare. 'Hush,' he told her, and crazily the mare stopped struggling for a little. She looked wild-eyed and as terrified as Benjy but maybe Ben's bedside manner was not bad for horses either.

But Lily had eyes only for Benjy. She sat as Ben was doing— the mud only sucked you in if there was a big weight on a small surface so she presented the mud with her backside. And prayed it was big enough. She was desperate to help but Ben had Benjy fast in his arms, fighting for the mud to give up its prize.

And it did. Slowly, gradually, Benjy was eased outward. Then, wonderfully, as his torso came free, the rest of him came in a rush and Ben sprawled backward, his arms full of mud and boy.

Lily reached for him but Ben wasn't relinquishing him. They lay in the mud, a tangle of legs and arms and mud and pure emotion. Ben's small shoulders were shaking with sobs and his face was a blotched and crumpled mess. He lay on Ben's chest while Lily reached out and ran her fingers through his hair and felt her heart go cold at the thought of what might have been.

'She kept pulling,' Benjy sobbed at them, still cradled against his father. 'I tried to take her to the nice grass but she wouldn't come. And she keeps sinking more.'

'Oh, Benjy. It'll be OK.'

'It's not OK,' Benjy managed, hiccuping on a sob. His small body might be crumpled against Ben, gathering comfort, but he was made of stern stuff, and he'd only slumped a little and now he was pulling away. 'She's stuck and we have to help her.' He bit his lip, trying valiantly not to cry any more.

Enough. This was her baby. Lily sat up and tugged him away from Ben, into her arms. 'Sweetheart, let's think about you first. We'll look after Flicker but we need to check you. Are you hurt? Were you kicked?'

'N-no. Just stuck.'

'So nothing hurts now.'

'My dad pulled me out of the mud,' Benjy whispered. 'So I'm OK.'

'It's what your dad does best,' Lily whispered back, holding him close. 'He's very, very good at making people OK. Just lucky we had him here, hey?'

There was a moment's silence. Lily very carefully didn't look at Ben—but it was a struggle.

'Tell us what happened,' Ben managed at last. He was sitting up too now, taking in the full mess the mare was in. Or maybe he was trying not to look at his son. He'd been rocked to the core, Lily thought, and she knew it because she was feeling exactly the same. The only difference was that she'd known she loved her son to bits.

Ben looked like a thunderbolt had hit him.

But Flicker needed them. Ben's question was waiting to be answered and finally Benjy took a deep breath and told them.

'Flicker was acting funny when Rosa and me came out this morning. She kept going back and forth by the gate, over and over. Rosa said maybe something's happening, but then the helicopter came and she said stay with Flicker and she went inside. And no one came and no one came and Flicker was going back and forth and back and forth and I thought I'd start taking her down to the river like she wants. 'Cos you'd know where I'd be. But she was still acting funny. She was whinnying and looking behind her all the time. And then she came the wrong way. She pulled and pulled and I couldn't stop her coming here. Then she got stuck and every time she fought I went deeper and I couldn't get out of the mud.' His words ended on a frightened whisper. Lily hugged him close and looked at Ben, who was watching them as if…

As if nothing.

'What can we do?' This was no time for wondering what Ben was thinking, she decided. She didn't have a clue. When had she ever?

'Let's check.' Ben edged forward, lying by the mare's flanks, keeping out of range of the churned mud at her head. She was still for the moment, but quivering in obvious fear. And pain? He ran his hand down her side and he frowned.

'Maybe she's in labour,' he said, and Lily winced and held Benjy tighter still. Mare stuck in mud. In labour?

'Throw us another complication, why don't you?' she demanded, and Ben managed a smile.

'Sorry. But let's assume the worst. We need equipment.'

What sort of equipment? Maybe putting the mare down was the kindest option, she thought bleakly. Oh, but Benjy…

'It's not time for that yet,' Ben said, his smile fading, and she knew he'd seen the bleakness of her thoughts. 'Benjy, I want you and your mother to stay here while I fetch what I need. I want you to stay calm and stay away from the churned-up mud, and I want you to try and keep Flicker calm as well. No more struggling. I'll be as fast as I can.'

He hesitated, then he moved back to where they sat and touched Benjy lightly on the cheek. Then, with the same muddy finger, he touched Lily. It was a feather touch and why the touch of a mud-caked finger should warm her—why it reassured her that all was well—she didn't know. But it did.

'Great beside manner,' she managed, and he smiled again.

'The doctor will make it all better,' he said. 'Just keep on believing that, you two. But the doctor had better move. I'll be back as soon as I can be. Stay calm.'

It was all very well staying calm and controlled when Ben was close, but the moment he disappeared it got a lot harder. But she was a doctor, too, Lily decided. So conjure up your own bedside manner, she told herself. Right!

'We have to stay calm,' she told Benjy sternly, and they both turned to looked at the mare. Her eyes were wild and fearful, and while they watched, Lily saw a ripple pass over her glossy hide. A muscle contraction? Labour?

Lily had been in some tricky delivery situations before but none surpassed this.

'Ben will know what to do,' she murmured, more to herself than to Benjy or Flicker. 'He's gone to get what we need.' What did they need? A crane? Did farms have cranes? She knew the answer to that would be no.

She reached out across the mud and touched the mare's nose, but Flicker snorted and flung back her head in alarm. 'It's OK, girl,' Lily told her, but maybe the mare heard the lack of certainty in her voice.

'I sang her a Kira song before you came,' Benjy whispered. 'She went down so far I thought she might go all the way. I was scared I'd be pulled down, too, and I didn't know what else to do so I just held onto her and sang.'

'That was a really sensible thing to do,' Lily said, swallowing hard at the thought of the bravery he'd shown. She thought of what sensible things she could do and she came up with only one suggestion. 'Do you think we could both sing?'

'OK,' Benjy said doubtfully. 'I will if you will.'

So they did, and it was dumb but it seemed to work. They sat on the soft ground in front of the mare—but not so close as to alarm her or be sucked down as well. Lily held Benjy on her knee and they sang together the songs Kira had taught both of them, soft island songs, meant to pacify a child before sleep. They were songs that were meant to murmur that all was right with the world and it was safe.

All wasn't right with her world, Lily thought, but Ben had saved her son and he'd save the horse as well—she knew it. So she held Benjy tight and she sang until finally Ben reappeared, driving the farm truck. He parked it just in front of where the ground became soft. While Lily and Benjy finished the song they'd started, he climbed from the cab and started unloading gear.

Planks. Lots and lots of wooden planks, each about six feet long. Spades. What looked like tarpaulins.

'Let's help,' Lily said, but Flicker tossed back her head, her eyes fearful again. 'Benjy, you keep singing while I go to help Ben. She's your friend.'

'OK,' Benjy said. 'But I'm scared.'

'Ben's here now. Flicker will be fine. The best person to be here in an emergency is an emergency doctor. You'll see.'

By the time she reached him, Ben had almost finished unloading. He smiled at Lily as she approached, the same way he might smile at a terrified patient.

'We'll get her out.'

'You're as worried as I am,' she accused, and he gave a rueful smile.

'I might be.'

'And if we can't get her out?'

'I've called the local vet for back-up.'

'And the local vet would be how local?'

'He's half an hour's drive away.'

'So he'll be here in half an hour?'

'Not quite. He'll be here half an hour after he delivers a heifer of her first calf.'

'Oh, great.'

'I brought the rifle,' he muttered, and Lily gulped. Um, that was never a back-up plan in her sort of medicine.

'It's only if she breaks anything or starts to struggle deeper,' he said.

'She can't deliver a foal where she is.'

'We don't know she's in labour.'

'I'm sure she's having contractions.'

'Right.' His lips compressed. 'So we get her out before she has her baby.'

'How?'

'Dig,' he said, and handed over a spade. 'We're in this together.'

They were.

They laid planks around the mare, giving themselves a solid place to work. Right. The next thing was to stop the mare sinking further. Ben knelt on one side of the mare and shoved a tarpaulin under her belly, talking softly to her all the time. Lily knelt on the other side.

Flicker's belly was resting on mud, sinking a little beneath the surface. Ben worked his way in from one side; Lily burrowed from the other; Flicker stayed still and they were able to drag the tarp through.

There were three more contractions as they worked.

'Now what?' Lily demanded, struggling to her feet again, a heap of mud coming with her.

'Now we dig,' Ben said. 'Benjy, you keep singing. You're exactly what Flicker needs. Lily, we're working down from about six feet in front of her, digging what will act as a ramp outward from her hooves. We'll be sliding planks in as we dig and then we'll cover them with canvas. She should be able to get purchase.'

'Really?'

'Got any other suggestions?'

'Nope,' Lily said, and started to dig.

They worked for half an hour, digging forward steadily. Lily wasn't half the digger Ben was, but every few minutes they swapped so the trench they were creating was even. Fifteen minutes into the digging, Lily had blisters on blisters but she would die rather than admit it. The thought of the rifle in the back of the truck was the best of spurs.

And all the time Benjy sang, in a high, quavery voice that held the occasional sob. Every time he paused, the horse became agitated again, rolling her eyes, pulling back. Her legs had no purchase in the mud and she'd almost ceased trying to get herself out, but Lily was worrying now about shock.

How did you tell if a horse was in shock?

'Can we contact the vet and see if we can give her a sedative?' she asked as she dug.

'I'm imagining a sedative will cross the placenta, the same as in human babies. Wouldn't you say?'

'Yes, but—'

'I already asked the vet,' Ben said grimly. 'No sedative. Let's just dig.'

So dig they did, forming a sloping hole downward, until they had what was essentially a ramp from close to the mare's front legs. They left about a foot of mud between the hole and the mare's legs, deciding they'd break through in one hit at the end, fearing she might lash out.

Finally the hole was dug. Swiftly they lined it with boards and covered the boards with canvas, shoving the canvas under the boards at the ends and the sides so as soon as the horse was on it, her weight would hold it in place.

'Now we just have to break through,' Ben muttered. 'Lily, hold her halter, talk to her, see if you can distract her.'

Ben didn't want to get kicked, Lily thought, and she was in complete agreement. Neither did he want her to surge forward when only one leg was free.

'OK, Benjy, we're into distraction.'

The mare was in obvious pain now. Labour must be advancing. Her eyes were panicked, and Lily thought it was more than being stuck that was panicking her.

She had to distract the mare from pain—and from Ben.

She knelt on the mud to the side of the mare and tugged Flicker's halter, making her look sideways rather than straight ahead.

'No struggling,' she said sternly. 'Benjy, tell your friend Ben's trying to help. Flicker, look at us.' She jerked the halter. 'Look at us.'

Ben was in the hole. He was scraping at the last of the mud, trying to break through. Nearly there. The last barrier of mud was collapsing down on itself, freeing the mare's legs.

Flicker appeared not to notice. Her eyes were looking inward. There was a foal in there, battling to come out.

'OK,' Ben muttered, and hauled himself up and onto the far side of the hole from Lily. He reached out and grabbed the other side of Flicker's halter. 'Let's get you out, gorgeous. Lily, pull.'

Lily staggered to her feet.

'Stand aside,' Ben ordered Benjy.

'Shall I sing?' Ben's face was a picture of bewilderment, fear and the beginnings of excitement.

'No,' Ben said. 'Get behind her and shout. As loud as you can.'

'Only her front feet are free,' Benjy said doubtfully, staring at Flicker's still trapped hindquarters, and Ben grimaced.

'I know,' he told Benjy. 'But she's a strong horse. It should be enough.'

It had to be enough, Lily thought, for to dig under the abdomen to free the back legs was impossible. It'd be impossible even if they had time. Which they didn't.

So Lily and Ben pulled and Benjy shouted. For a long moment Lily thought the mare simply wasn't going to try. There'd be so many sensations hammering the mare now that being stuck in mud would be the least of them. But Lily pulled as if she really believed the mare would come free and Ben pulled, too. Flicker suddenly hauled a foreleg upward, the mud squelching as it released its grip. One hoof hit the canvas-covered wood and found purchase. Encouraged, she tried the second hoof and it, too, found purchase.

'Now for the big pull,' Ben murmured. 'Come on, my beauty.'

'Please,' Lily muttered. 'Please.'

And then it happened. The mare gave one last despairing whinny, found purchase with both hooves and hauled herself forward, with a movement so sudden that Lily sprawled backward in the mud. Ben didn't stop. The mare was lurching out onto the boards, and Ben was tugging the mare forward, further, further, leading her as fast as he could over the soft ground so she couldn't sink again. While Lily lay in the mud and tried to regain her breath, man and horse made it to the pasture.

Safe.

Lily lay on the mud and watched them, and smiled and smiled. Benjy came up to her, worried about why she hadn't risen, and she tugged him down and held him tight and grinned.

'Wasn't that the best?'

'You're covered in mud. Just like me.'

'And I love it. Just like I love you.'

'Oi!' On dry ground Ben was holding the mare's head and looking back at them in bemusement. 'Benjy, could you remind your mother that she's a doctor. We have a baby to deliver, guys, so if you're finished wallowing in the mud, maybe you could help.'

* * *

What they needed was a nice easy delivery but, of course, that wasn't going to happen. Flicker was exhausted and distressed to begin with and she hardly had the strength to push.

But Ben had thought past getting the mare out of the mud. He'd filled a couple of huge Thermos flasks with hot water and he'd tossed buckets and rags and rope into the back of the truck.

'Practically a whole birthing unit,' Lily noted. 'But no incubator?'

'The sun's incubator enough,' Ben growled. 'If we can get it out.' He glanced at Benjy, who was starting to look distressed again. 'I meant if we can get it out quickly. Benjy, do you think you can keep these buckets full of clean water? If you took one over to the river and half filled it, then we'd have it ready. We'll top it up with hot water from the Thermos. That way we can have as much warm, soapy water as we need. Stay on the firmer ground where there are rocks to walk on. Don't go anywhere near where we've been digging.'

'Sure,' Benjy said, desperate to be doing something to help.

Lily was the same. She stood in the sun, the mud drying hard on her body, and felt like she needed direction.

It was Flicker doing the work.

'Hold her head,' Ben ordered, so she did. Ben cleaned the mare down a little, washing away the worst of the mud. The mare submitted to his ministrations with uneasy patience. She kept looking behind her as if she couldn't figure what was hurting. And then what must have been a deeper contraction hit. She whinnied a little and sank to her knees, then rolled onto her side.

'Where's the vet?' Lily demanded nervously, as Benjy lugged over his fourth bucketful of water.

'Why do we need a vet?' Ben asked.

'How long do horse labours last?'

'I have no idea. But let's not panic yet.'

'I can't think of anything else to do.'

'There speaks a thoroughly competent doctor.'

'You went to the same medical school,' she snapped. 'So what are you doing that is useful? Any minute you'll tell me to go help Benjy.'

'It's better than you both pacing the waiting room,' he retorted. 'Maybe you could go buy some cigars.'

'Or maybe I can just pace,' she muttered. 'Hurry up, Flicker.'

'I'd reckon she's doing the best she can.'

'How would you know?'

'And how would you?' They glared at each other and Ben put his head on one side and surveyed her, a strange smile behind his eyes.

'You're beautiful when you're panicking.'

'Shut up and deliver a foal.'

'There's no—'

But his words were cut short. The mare gave a mighty heave. A gush of water flowed, followed seconds later by a tiny hoof.

'Two hooves?' Lily murmured. 'Come on.'

Another contraction. No second hoof.

Another contraction.

No hoof.

'There has to be,' Ben muttered, worried, and Lily guessed what he wanted before he said it. She emptied a Thermos into the closest bucket, then swished soap round in it, handing the cake to Ben. It couldn't be harder than a human baby. Could it?

Ben was already soaping his arm. He felt around the tiny hoof and then had to pause until another contraction had passed.

Now.

But it wasn't now.

'My hand's too big,' he gasped. 'I'm not as sure of what I'm looking for as I am in human birth. You try.'

She was already soaping. She knelt, then figured she was

still too high so she lay full length on the ground and waited for the next contraction to pass.

'Ease back, Flicker,' Ben told the mare. 'Breathe for a bit.'

'I bet she skipped prenatal classes,' Lily muttered. 'Irresponsible ladies…'

And then the contraction was past. Lily soaped her hand some more, then carefully slid her fingers past the one tiny hoof.

Where…? Come on….

Her fingers found another hoof.

Fantastic. There had to be a nose, she thought, and then wondered if it was a front hoof or a back hoof. Did horses come out forward or backward? Was that a nose she was feeling? Whatever, she shoved her fingers as far back as she could, hooked the tiny hoof and hauled it toward her.

Another contraction hit. Her hand was still trapped. She gasped in pain, the sensation that of a vice against her hand. 'Yike,' she muttered. 'Yike, yike, yike…'

'Benjy,' Ben was yelling, calling to Benjy to leave his final bucket of water and come back. 'We think the foal's coming.'

'I know what's coming,' she muttered. 'She's delivering my arm. Don't you dare call Benjy.'

'Why—'

'My language,' she yelled, as another contraction rolled through. 'Block your ears.'

The hoof had slithered through her fingers and wasn't forward enough, but now she had it again. This time she tugged with more certainty. Heaven knew if it was right but it had to come in her direction so why not aim it that way? She just had it where she wanted it when the next contraction hit.

Her hand lifted free. The second hoof appeared like magic. With a nose.

And then…and then a foal slithered slowly out into a brand-new world.

* * *

It had been a huge physical effort, as well as an emotional one. Ben looked on as Benjy examined the perfect little foal. The little boy burst into tears and was gathered into his mother's arms and held.

Ben cleared the foal's nose and lifted the tiny creature round to his mother's head so Flicker could nuzzle her baby then lie there in exhausted contentment.

Lily had been lying full length during the foal's birth and she'd now rolled sideways to give Ben room to work. But she was going nowhere. She hugged Benjy to her as he sobbed and sobbed, and Ben thought this was much more than a foal being born. This was a culmination of all that had gone before—a month of hell.

Or more than that.

He looked down at Lily, bloodstained, filthy, smiling through her tears, holding her son against her breast, cradling him to her, whispering nothings.

He loved her.

He loved them all, he thought. Flicker and foal. Rosa and Doug.

Benjy. His son.

And Lily.

He always had, he thought, and it was such a massive, light-bulb moment that he felt his world shift in some momentous way that he didn't understand.

But his world hadn't moved from its axis. It was as if it had settled back onto an axis that he hadn't known had been missing.

He thought back to something Benjy had said.

My dad pulled me out of the mud, Benjy had whispered. *So I'm OK.*

His son had needed him and he'd been there. If Benjy needed him again, how could he not be close?

If Lily needed him… It was exactly the same.

And more. He thought then that it was more than him being needed. Because what he felt for them both was a need itself.

He needed them both. They might need him but he needed them so desperately that he could never again walk away.

He hadn't been there for Bethany, he thought, thinking suddenly of his baby sister. It hadn't been his fault. He hadn't been permitted to be there. But he'd loved her and now suddenly the grief for her loss settled, as if something had been explained that had been tormenting him for years.

He'd loved Bethany. It was OK to grieve for her. She wasn't…nothing.

And with that thought the guilt he'd been carrying for years suddenly, inexplicably, eased.

Today he'd been there for his son. He'd been there for Lily and he would be again, for ever and ever, as long as they both lived.

He needed them. This was his family.

You are my north and my south.

Who'd said that? He'd heard it at a funeral, he remembered. It had been the wife of a sergeant killed in East Timor. The woman had stood dry-eyed and empty, talking to her lost love.

You are my north and my south.

He'd hardly listened. He remembered hearing the words and then consciously deciding that he needed to think about what he was doing the next day. He couldn't let himself dwell on it.

Because love like that was terrible.

Only it wasn't. He'd only thought it was terrible.

Today Benjy had called him Dad.

Sure, it might end, he thought as he looked down at his woman and his son. The thought of that was empty, bleak as hell, yet what he'd been doing until now was just as bleak.

To do without that love because one day it might end—

that was dumb. He could see it now with a clarity that almost blew him away.

'It's not just you,' he said to Lily, breaking in on the conversation to himself halfway through. 'It's more than just you.'

Lily looked up at him, smiling past her son's rumpled curls.

'It's not just me?'

'I do love Doug and Rosa.'

'How about that?' she whispered, and smiled at him.

It was enough. He sank to his knees and stooped to kiss her. But she had her arms full of child and his kiss went awry, as it had to in these crazy circumstances, but, then, he knew his intention.

And maybe she did, too. For she was still smiling, her eyes full of unshed tears but the beginnings of joy not far behind.

'I need you,' he told her. 'Lily, I've always needed you. I've just been too stupid to see. But what happened today… We're a family. I know I don't deserve a second chance but I'm asking you for one. I want to marry you. I want to adjust our lives so we can be together. But I never want to be apart again.'

'Oh, Ben…'

'Will you come and live on our island?' Benjy asked, absorbing Ben's words and heading straight to what mattered most.

'Yes,' he said, and watched as Lily's eyes filled with tears.

'Ben, we can't ask you…'

'You're not asking. I'm telling. I'm coming home.' He bent forward and kissed her on the nose, and then, more surely, he kissed her on the mouth. When they finally broke away they were all smiling and Benjy's was the biggest smile of all.

'Kisses are yucky but I liked that,' he said.

'Great,' Ben told him. 'It's good that you like it because I intend to kiss your mother just like that every day for the rest of our lives. Once first thing in the morning, once just before we go to sleep and a hundred times in between.'

'We have a happy ending,' Lily whispered.

'I don't believe in endings.'

'No?'

'No.'

'I think this morning…' he told her as he gathered woman and child into his arms and held them tight. 'I think this morning is a happy beginning. Benjy, do you know what a phosphorescent tide is?'

'No,' said Benjy, puzzled.

'It's when the lights go on in the sea,' he said. 'In shallow water it might happen once in a lifetime. Your mother and I saw it but you missed out. So I've decided. I need to come back to your island so we can watch out together for phosphorescent tides. I have a feeling that when we're around, the concept of once in a lifetime is ridiculous. We've been given a second chance, and from now, from right at this minute, we're going to take any chance we're given.'

CHAPTER TWELVE

THE first anniversary of the insurrection on the island could well have been a day of sadness, but the islanders of Kapua had never looked on death as a final farewell. Funerals were a time of celebration, of affirmation of the power of life. They were a thanksgiving for the joy of life itself.

But the shock of the attempted coup had thrown the islanders off course. The funerals twelve months ago had been blurred with horror. Now, a year later, the islanders wanted to do it better. They'd come to terms with their losses in their own way, and they wished to right a wrong—to celebrate the lives of those they'd lost and to turn mourning into a peaceful acceptance and a deep thankfulness for lives well lived. Those killed by Jacques's accomplices had been loved, and that love would live for ever in the hearts of those left behind. And of those to come.

That was the gist of the words spoken by the island's pastor on this day of remembrance. Everyone on the island was there. The soft sea breeze blew gently across the graveyard, and the scent of frangipani mixed with the salt from the sea.

Lily stayed in the background, with Benjy by her side. On the other side of Benjy, holding his hand, letting the child lean against him, stood his father. Her husband.

Ben and Benjy. Her family.

She listened to the pastor's words, and let the peace of acceptance drift into her heart. 'Thank you for loving me,' she told Kira, and she glanced across at her husband and she smiled. 'And thank you for bringing Ben back home to me.'

For Ben was truly home now. He was an accepted islander. Lily's husband. Benjy's father. The islanders had accepted him into their hearts with nothing but pleasure.

And why would they not have? In less than a year Ben had transformed the medical set-up on the island. There were remote clinics on each of the outer islands, with rapid transfer available to the main base on Kapua. And the base at Kapua was wonderful. The tiny hospital had been extended to double its size. Lily was based there now, as were two interns on rotation from Sydney. And Sam... That had been a coup in itself. For when the time had come for Sam to leave he'd looked long and hard at the island—and at Pieter's pretty teacher daughter—and he'd decided that maybe Kapua wasn't such a bad place to put down roots.

So there were now five doctors on the island, and maybe there'd be even more when the new wing of the hospital opened. The obstetric wing.

It was magic, Lily thought as she continued to listen. From an island with basic medical facilities, they were moving fast to be state of the art.

Her island home had become even more of a paradise.

Not that they stayed there all the time now. In the few days after Doug's heart attack, when Lily and Ben and Benjy had been marooned, caring for a newborn foal but with little else to do but talk, and nothing to talk about but their future, they'd worked it out. Doug and Rosa would be grandparents to Benjy. They'd been practically all the parents that Ben had known and grandparents couldn't be left out of the equation of this embryonic family. Therefore four times a year they'd spend at least a week at the farm, and four times a year Doug and Rosa would be flown out to the island to spend as long as they wanted there.

They were there now. After his double bypass Doug looked and felt wonderful. Doug and Pieter had struck up a fast friendship, and Doug and Gualberto were as thick as thieves. Many more of the islanders would end up as visitors back at the farm, Lily thought happily. Her world had been extended and was about to be extended even more.

But first… There were ghosts to be laid to rest. First loves to be acknowledged.

The pastor had finished speaking now. Flowers had been laid on each grave, and the islanders were drifting away. There'd be a celebration on the beach tonight, but for now individual families needed time to themselves to assimilate all they'd felt that day.

Rosa and Doug were moving from the graveyard, too, but before they left Rosa reached into her capacious bag and produced a box. She smiled across at Lily, in her eyes a question, and Lily left her husband and son to take the box from her.

'What is it?' Ben asked as she returned.

She looked up at this wonderful man she loved with all her heart, and she thought, Was this the right thing to do? She'd done it without asking. She and Rosa had done it without talking to him about it because they knew this would hurt. They wanted the hurt to be brief but they also knew that unfinished business must be completed before moving forward.

'It's Bethany's ashes,' she said, and she saw his face become blank with shock.

'Bethany…'

'Rosa said you weren't permitted to go to her funeral. She said as far as she knew your parents hadn't ever told you where she was. Doug remembered a fight when you were about eight—you asking what had happened and your father saying to leave it, the dead were best forgotten.'

'Doug and Rosa always thought it was wrong,' she whispered. 'Only they never knew what to do—how to broach it with you. But after we married, Rosa talked to me about it. She knew that Bethany had been cremated. She knew her ashes had been left in a memorial wall at a huge Sydney cemetery. She'd always hated the thought. So…' She faltered a little then, looking at the blankness on his face, hoping she'd done right.

'We wrote to the accountant who was the executor of your parents' estate,' she whispered. 'We asked if we needed your permission but he said you'd never been involved—that as far as he knew you didn't even know where Bethany's ashes were. But he was happy to sign a release form. Because we thought… Rosa and Doug and I thought that you should bring Bethany home. We thought maybe you could scatter her ashes here. Or maybe you could scatter them at the farm. Wherever. But we thought we'd like to help you to do that.' She faltered. 'Ben, If you want us to take the ashes back to Sydney then we will. But Rosa and Doug and I thought…we thought this might be right.'

The blankness faded as Ben stared down at the box, thinking through what they'd done. His gaze lifted, meeting hers. Beside him, Benjy stood watchful. Lily had explained to Benjy who Bethany was. Kira's death had made Benjy more mature than his years. He knew enough now to be silent, and he knew this moment was important. He held Ben's hand and Lily thought that this was right. Ben was holding his son as he thought about a little sister he'd loved a long time ago yet had never said farewell to.

'I love you,' Ben whispered.

'I know,' Lily replied, trying to hold back tears. 'But Bethany was your first love. Benjy and I would like to be with you while you say goodbye, but if you don't want us…'

'Of course I want you.' He tugged Benjy closer and hugged him. 'You know that. You know how much.'

She did. The world settled a little. This was the right thing to do, Lily thought, feeling a sense of peace and absolution sweep over her.

She held out the box to him, then gestured to Benjy. Benjy came to her as Ben took his sister's ashes in both his hands.

'If you want to do it here, now, the pastor is waiting,' Lily told him. 'And Rosa and Doug are just through the trees. They loved Bethany, too. They'd also like the chance to say goodbye.'

'Yes,' he said softly, and then more firmly, 'Yes. This is a good time to do this. The best.'

So this memorial service became the memorial service for one other. The pastor came forward quietly and said a prayer and a blessing, and Ben opened the box and scattered his sister's ashes over the wildflowers of the churchyard; over the graves of those who had gone before; over the calm and lovely headland of this, their island home.

And when it was over, they turned and walked together, Ben and Lily, with Benjy walking behind between Rosa and Doug. A family going home.

'It was the best thing,' Ben told her, holding her close. 'To let me say goodbye…'

'It's a lovely name, Bethany,' Lily whispered. Her hand was warm in his, secure, loved. 'Do you think we should consider using it again?'

'For…'

'For a new little life,' she whispered, and she smiled and held his hand tighter. 'Today we've said goodbye to some of our family, my darling Ben, but in a seven months' time…time to say hello.'

That night, in the waves around Kapua, the tiny phosphorescent creatures came again.

The lights went on in their sea.

Miracles happened.

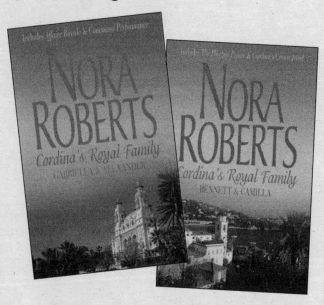

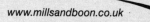

FREE

4 BOOKS AND A SURPRISE GIFT!

We would like to take this opportunity to thank you for reading this Mills & Boon® book by offering you the chance to take FOUR more specially selected titles from the Medical Romance™ series absolutely FREE! We're also making this offer to introduce you to the benefits of the Mills & Boon® Reader Service™—

- ★ **FREE home delivery**
- ★ **FREE gifts and competitions**
- ★ **FREE monthly Newsletter**
- ★ **Books available before they're in the shops**
- ★ **Exclusive Reader Service offers**

Accepting these FREE books and gift places you under no obligation to buy; you may cancel at any time, even after receiving your free shipment. Simply complete your details below and return the entire page to the address below. You don't even need a stamp!

YES! Please send me 4 free Medical Romance books and a surprise gift. I understand that unless you hear from me, I will receive 6 superb new titles every month for just £2.80 each, postage and packing free. I am under no obligation to purchase any books and may cancel my subscription at any time. The free books and gift will be mine to keep in any case.

M7ZEE

Ms/Mrs/Miss/Mr..Initials ....
BLOCK CAPITALS PLEASE

Surname ....

Address ....

....

....Postcode ....

Send this whole page to:
The Reader Service, FREEPOST CN81, Croydon, CR9 3WZ